The Belcher

Overserved Underdog

By Luke Schmaltz

ISBN: 978-1-7356458-0-3

Audiobook and eBook versions available at lukeschmaltz. com.

Published in partnership with Mutiny Press
2 S. Broadway
Denver, CO. 80209
mutinyinfocafe.com

Cover art by Jef Kopp

Special editorial thanks to Matthew Kenneth Yoss, Charles Augustus Steen III, Frank Kelly Rich and Gene Pinson.

For Christal

Chapter One

A Rumbling Within

Earl Danners opened his gullet and poured down the fifth beer of the night. He could feel himself beginning to relax — no longer strained by the anxiety of being socially inept. He stood up, untucked his red flannel shirt from his faded blue jeans and slumped back down over the stick. A scruffy mop of blondish-brown hair spilled over his collar, around his ears and partially down into his face. His bangs were camouflage – or so he thought.

By now, the bartenders at The Joker knew the routine. His finished beers were deliberately left in front of him like chess pieces scattered across an invisible board. As he arranged each emptied bottle among the others, a fresh one was twisted open with a *"fssst"* and placed before him without discourse or blather.

Earl liked to hunker down at the end of the bar, past the elbow-shaped corner and against the far wall near the broken ATM machine. He regarded each vessel before him as an ally, a silent sentinel that had played an integral role in his fleeting fulfillment. The more company he amassed onto the bar top before him, the better he felt. He was among friends at last, and tonight was turning out to be quite a party.

The bar was alive with activity, as several dozen people crowded up against the long curving length of wood and mashed in among one another, ignoring an empty dance floor a few feet away that was the sole witness to Jimmy Sensitive and the Bedwetters as they slogged through their last song of hip, ironic pop. Some were yammering so close to their friends' heads they could have reached out with their tongues and licked their earlobes. Just about everyone was yapping at once, as though this was their last moment alive to unburden themselves from a terrible secret. Drinks rose and descended, mouths opened and closed, slurred voices swirled around one another as neon light glinted off the moist luster of eyeballs and saliva-covered teeth. It was a masquerade orchestrated by chaos — the choreography of human madness with no conductor and no exemptions.

Earl was perplexed by the allure of social gatherings and wondered why crowds of people attract more of the same. He was even a little happy to be a part of it all even though he was more of a spectator than a participant. He cared deeply about the wellbeing of others without understanding why, yet, he feared other people because he knew that each could express the cruel gene of betrayal that was stamped into all human DNA.

Amid the din swayed the feminine curves of a figure he had long since memorized. Rumor had it that her real name was Daphne something-or-other, but everyone called her Cricket, and in a world of hideous threes and frumpy fours … she was easily an 11. Earl assumed she was of drinking age, maybe a few years older but her swagger gave her a threatening air of authority. There was always a group of guys orbiting around her, strategizing like scavengers on how

2

to get close … but none of them ever did, including Earl. He didn't dare, as he simply lacked the social skills required to make conversation with a gorgeous young woman.

Her routine was always the same. She would march through the door, the sleet glimmering off her vinyl pants, leather jacket and jet-black shoulder length hair. She would order a double shot of tequila, slam it in one gulp, leave a fat tip and then lean there — gripping the edge of the bar — swaying side to side. The swaying would gradually diminish and then she would freeze, wait for several moments, let out a blood curdling scream and then bolt out the door like a feral cat.

He was 13 beers in when the unmistakable screech of a barstool scooting across a hardwood floor pierced through the music and barroom chatter.

"Get the fuck away from me, asshole!" a voice screamed. It was one of the Denver Derelicts, a fledgling "motorcycle gang" of fringe dwellers who were mostly too broke or incompetent to actually own a bike.

The yelling continued, "I swear to God I'll fucking kill you!" The biker was known as Roach — a menacing brute with neck tattoos, a leather vest over a jean jacket, chains, clunky rings on every finger — the whole bit. His side-kick, Skeeter, had a shaved head with the image of a skull drilled into the side of it. Roach was towering over one of the neighborhood regulars who was swaddled in a mamma's boy scarf and tucked into an oversized newsboy hat. It was Earl's guess that the hip guy was hammered drunk and he bumped into Roach — spilling the man's booze.

The crowd moved away as The Roach shoved the guy down onto the floor. He got up – confused – and Skeeter grabbed him by the back of the head and bashed his head against the bar. As he cried for help Earl stood up, unsure of what to do.

The guy came barreling down the bar headfirst like a ragdoll thrown by an ape and smashed into Earl's collection of bottles.

Earl felt a wave of rage was about to erupt within him. "Goddammit. I'm just sitting here minding my own business," he thought.

Earl was always the guy to slink off to the sidelines to grit his teeth in hesitation and disgust when trouble came stomping down the center aisle. But, 27 years of silence, two-and-a-half decades of fear and millions of moments of confusion finally colluded within him — along with the car-bonation of 156 ounces of beer.

He was going to try to yell something like "hey" or "knock it off," but instead, a dense rumbling began in his abdomen that quickly grew to a resonant growl and then exploded into a thunderous ear-splitting roar that sounded like a throttling 747 turbofan engine with a chamber full of birds being hacked apart by the rotor blades. He belched a mighty tsunami of sonic power that swept every can and glass off the bar while every hat, scarf and pair of thick-rimmed glasses went flying backwards along with those who were no longer wearing them.

Everyone who was positioned directly in front of Earl was suddenly sprawled across the floor several feet away. Roach and Skeeter arose first, pulled out their knives and began to approach Earl. He reached for his beer, took a slug, and then unleashed a belch that lifted the Derelicts up off their feet and tossed them through the air. They both crashed through the pane glass window facade and landed prone in the street.

He swayed before them as they looked up — everyone sharing a moment of mutual disbelief. Roach pulled a 357 Magnum from inside his vest and pointed it at Earl's face as bystanders began screaming and running for cover. He pulled the trigger as Earl belched again. It was a sonic wave powerful enough to alter the bullet's trajectory by warping the space between the barrel and Earl's forehead. Rather than splitting his skull in two, the bullet veered off at an angle and shattered the front glass of the jukebox. One Bourbon, One Scotch, One Beer by George Thorogood continued to play as Earl stepped around overturned tables and chairs then through the plate glass window frame, past stupefied tough guys laying on their backsides and he staggered off into the night.

Chapter Two

A Man in a Hat

The next morning, Earl shuffled into the Denver Public Library and clocked in 11 minutes late. After busting up The Joker in a beer-basted haze, he spiraled into a frenzy of anxiety and disbelief at the sort of decimation that erupted from his esophagus. In order to get to sleep he had to down five more beers. As he was swaying in front of the mirror just before passing out, he absentmindedly belched, and the glass splintered into a web of shards.

His hangover was profound, but since he rarely spoke to his coworkers his late arrival went unnoticed by everyone except for his supervisor, Wendell. Those beady little eyes homed in on him from behind thick, woozy lenses set into pretentious black-rimmed frames. Earl pretended not to notice as Wendell straightened his bow tie, cleared his throat and twitched in disapproval in his tight argyle sweater.

Earl set to the task of wheeling the recent returns cart about the premises, placing books back into their respective slots on the shelves. The inevitable waves of nausea began rolling through him. It was just a matter of time before he would have to bolt to the restroom and purge.

Trembling and turning green, he grabbed the toilet on either side and hurled a frothy mixture of beer and bile. "Whatever you do," he mumbled, "don't belch." He mused to himself about the efficiency of the barfing mechanism — how the smell of your own puke makes you puke even more. "It's a vicious cycle," he thought.

He leaned over the sink, wiping the vomit off his chin — trying to compose himself enough to get back to work. A gruff voice pierced the solace of the men's room — echoing off the tiled floor and walls and reverberating around Earl's ears. "Jesus boy, you look like you got eaten by a coyote and shit off a cliff."

Earl turned to face a substantial man leaning against the wall between the pissers deftly rolling a joint in fingerless, frayed leather gloves. He was well over six feet tall, wearing a tattered brown duster and a wide-brim cowboy hat.

"The name's Vasquez, Pablo Vasquez."

The man squinted as though he was suppressing laughter, or perhaps wincing from some sort of terrible pain. Earl didn't care to find out which, so he turned on his heels and split.

"Well shit ... it's just like I thought. This kid's a goddamn pussy."

Chapter Three

The Soothsayer

Earl staggered from the bathroom, found his cart of returned books and continued on with his task. People like this Pablo Vasquez guy were commonplace in the DPL. As a Federally operated property, it was illegal for library personnel to refuse admittance to just about anyone. So, vagrants, panhandlers and vagabonds lurking about the premises spewing unwanted commentary was part of the gig.

An hour later while placing *Creative Mythology - The Masks of God* by Joseph Campbell into its slot, he heard the gravelly voice again, "You should take that brick of a book back down and read it."

Earl turned away from the voice and continued down the aisle toward the Ds. "Hey, asshole" Pablo sneered, "ain't you sick of trying to be invisible?"

Earl paused and looked back at his pursuer. He noted the long, scraggly hair protruding from beneath the wide-brim hat, the thick mustache and deep-set, piercing brown eyes.

"Sir," Earl rasped in a tiny voice, "I don't want any trouble, OK?"

"Too late," said Pablo. "Nobody ever really wants trouble except for drama queens, shit talkers and bear pokers. But, since you ain't none of the above you can consider this your unlucky week, cuz it seems that trouble has found you."

"Hey look man if you're from the bar I'll be glad to pay for the, the, the ..."

"Shut the fuck up and listen."

"There's something mighty peculiar going on, and right now you and I are the only ones who know it. All those shitbags from last night just think whoever busted up the place was some psycho on meth or PCP. There was too much noise and flailing around for anyone to understand that a wallflower like you was the one harboring enough hate to turn the capitol building inside out. The pigs are all out looking for rival gang members of the Derelicts. The Nitwits or The Dumbshits or The Boar Tits — whatever, so don't get your underwear in a wad. I'd say you're off the radar. For now."

"What do you want?"

"Just ringin' out a warning. Now that you broke the seal and got a hint of what payback tastes like, it's gonna be hard for you to keep your yap shut, at least after you've had a few beers." Pablo lit a joint and continued "It's like my daddy used to say to me 'one of these days that mouth of yours is gonna get you in trouble, boy.'"

"How do you know —"

"I was sittin' right across from you at the other end of the bar, you fucktard. But you were too damn busy feeling sorry for yourself behind a wall of beer bottles that you failed to take account of your surroundings."

"Uuuhhh —"

"Quit your muttering and listen. This ability of yours is the trouble I'm talking about. Just cuz you ain't ready for it don't mean that its time hadn't come. It's gonna rear its head again and at some point, you're gonna have to make a choice: whether or not to squander your talent because you are a pussy or to stand up and belch like a man."

The smell of marijuana smoke was attracting the attention of the visitors and the library staff.

Wendell the supervisor and his bottle-bottom spectacles were approaching fast. "Hey mister, you'd better put that thing out. This is a no smo —"

"Aww button your lip you tie wearing dip," Pablo barked. "I prefer this indulgence — it's just a little pot, you think you have importance, but alas you do not." Wendell seemed to skid to a halt in his tracks. Pablo took a massive hit that he seemed to pull on for the better part of a minute while the floor manager fiddled with his glasses and tried to mutter commands of authority. The cherry burned down the length of the joint until it singed the callused skin of Pablo's thumb and forefinger. Then, he began to chant in a steady cadence without exhaling the smoke.

*"Words are a treasure and prose is a wonder
If ye seek only pleasure your mind turns to plunder"*

Wisps of smoke began to ascend from the corners of his mouth as his voice began to amplify. Everyone within earshot became paralyzed as he continued.

*"In the house of silence your mind must make thunder
Lest your freedom to dream be ravaged asunder"*

Pablo exhaled a massive wave of white smoke that washed out across the library floor and swirled around bookshelves and the heads of people frozen mid-stride. Earl tried to move but the hypnotizing hum emanating from Pablo's smoldering chant rendered him motionless.

Two-and-a-half minutes later, Earl, Wendell and the rest of the library floor inhabitants began to reanimate. They choked, hacked and waved their hands about trying to clear away the thick cloud of weed fog. When it finally dissipated and everyone regained their senses, Pablo was gone.

Chapter Four

The Gasser

The next day, Earl needed to try and clear his head, so he opted for some fresh air. Since it was his day off, he headed not for the street, but for the service elevator that would take him to the roof of his apartment building.

He looked out west over the skyline. He could spot at least a dozen construction cranes without even scanning left or right. Legal marijuana, big oil and gas and yet another tech boom were attracting hordes of transplants. Denver was quickly being transformed from an adolescent-sized cow town into an economic powerhouse. Not all the new residents, however, were goody two-shoes yuppies heralding the sterile wave of right-angled, brightly lit gentrification. With all herds come the bad and the ugly, and this migration was nothing short of grotesque. For every dozen or so white-toothed yuppies who moseyed into town under the speed limit, at least one or two bleary-eyed gamers came careening along after midnight with porn on the brain and a shirt full of potato chip crumbs.

The past 36 hours seemed like a terrible drug trip, and

all Earl wanted to do was to exhale a lung load of the crisp Colorado air and make it all fizzle away like a bad dream. As good as the breeze felt 18 stories up, that was clearly not happening. "That's it," he muttered, trying to wipe the fog from his brain by rubbing his temples. "I've finally lost it."

On the way back down to his apartment, the elevator stopped at the 10th floor. A man wearing grimy brown coveralls stepped in. He was holding a stretch of PVC conduit in one hand and a set of channel locks in the other. Earl assumed he was a plumber on a maintenance call to one of the apartment units. The guy had a shiny black beard with peculiar white strips descending from each corner of his mouth that met at a point a few inches below his chin. "Just like a skunk," Earl thought.

"How's it going?" asked the maintenance guy.

"Any idea how to fix a bad trip?" Earl's shyness made him a novice at flippancy, but he felt strangely liberated by recent events.

"Don't have anything like that now, but I'd say about 10 years ago I did. Stay away from that shit, man. It'll fuck up your intestines."

The maintenance guy chuckled a bit, then the time-halting awkwardness of the proverbial elevator ride next to a stranger sunk in. As the car approached the ground floor at a snail's pace, Earl noticed that the maintenance guy seemed like he was trembling — as though he was choking or maybe suppressing a laugh.

"You Ok?" Earl creaked.

"Pppppppfffffaaaahhh haaaaa ha ha ha ha," the maintenance man erupted in a barrage of laughter. Between guffaws he thrust out a fart that sounded like a toad being slowly backed over by a two-ton truck — a sickly croak of intestinal mustard gas with shrub-choking toxicity. The stench was like freshly sliced Limburger cheese basted in vulture vomit. It attacked Earl's nostrils like vaporized venom, and he went limp, falling forward and bonking his head on the elevator door as it opened. As he was passing out, he noted that the maintenance man was skipping away snickering, and each bounce of his feet was accentuated with a resounding toot that sounded like puffs out of a sewage-dipped kazoo.

Meanwhile, the elevator door was trying to close — only it was being stopped repeatedly by Earl's obstructing skull.

Chapter Five

If at First You Don't Succeed

Later that night, Earl skulked down Broadway wondering about his gastrointestinal condition, the library dope smoker in the hat and that farting freak in the elevator. LSD and psilocybin had played a big part in his teen years as he tried to skirt social anxiety, boredom and ire. Perhaps the last few days were the elaborately detrimental effects of too much tripping. He ducked into Jackknife Liquors and approached the beer coolers. Just before reaching in to grab a twelver of cheap asylum, the voice in his head chimed in, "Maybe I should lay off the sauce for a while. Shit's been getting weird lately." Instead of his routine purchase he opted for soda pop. At the register the store owner, Kim, looked at him quizzically. "Why you no dlink beer toonieet? You no feewing good?" Earl smiled almost imperceptibly and shook his head. He had been coming here for years, but he had never once exchanged words with Kim beyond the normal grunts and mumbles of retail interaction.

"I'm having a bad week" he warbled. The words felt weird — like they didn't belong in the air at first, but once they evaporated, he felt a strange urge to replace them with more. He pondered as he paid, then he trudged out the door. Kim watched him leave, "That the fust time I eva hear dat guy tawk" he mused.

Back at home, Earl tore into the soda hoping that the carbonated liquid would affect him as he hoped. An hour later he arranged six empty cans into a pyramid on the coffee table. He inhaled, intentionally swallowing some air to catalyze a belch that would confirm that what happened the night before was indeed just an anomaly. He felt the oxygen and carbon dioxide in his gut collude into a gaseous pocket that rose up and chambered in his chest like a live round at the base of a shotgun barrel. He clenched his fists, closed his eyes and pushed. The belch erupted with the familiar repetitive clap of his esophagus quickly opening and closing — but there was no sonic blast. The soda cans just stood there silently mocking him "Ha ha dummy! It's all in your head, and now you're so full of caffeine you'll never get to sleep … sucker!"

Back at Jackknife Liquors he stood in front of Kim at the checkout counter, this time with a 12 pack of Beer City's Best and the impending plan to drink himself to sleep. Again. "Ah hah! I knew you come back!" Kim sang. The weird urge to talk nagged at Earl's insides again. He felt the words forming, almost on their own.

"I'm still thirsty."

Kim threw his head back and laughed with abandon, then smiled like a ring-toss stand attendant at a county fair as he handed Earl his change. "You funny moddafucka!" he beamed.

Chapter Six

Beers in the Park

Earl walked back home the long way, taking Broadway north to Speer Blvd and then veering left towards the Sunken Gardens — one of Denver's partially kempt urban swathes where you could safely jog along a paved path by day and get mugged and left for dead in the shrubs by night. He sat on a swing — an oversize figure slumped over in a structure designed for children. Meanwhile, the cool October moonlight spilled his shadow across the sand to his right as he eased into the routine of steadily devouring a dozen beers. He was five cans in when a motorcycle boot stepped into the head of his shadow. "It ain't smart to drank alone," a voice taunted. "Folks say if you drink all by your lonesome that means you gots a problem. It looks to me like you gots a problem." Earl look up from his trance and noticed the red "D" patch on the front of the guy's leather vest, along with a few other familiar things like a skull tattooed on the side of the guy's head standing next to him.

"Do you repeat everything you say because you think it sounds cool, or because your friend here is too stupid to understand it the first time?" Earl was shocked that his hateful smartass thoughts were starting to fly out of his mouth untethered.

"I know you think you're hot shit — lighting off them M-80s in the bar the other night," Roach whined. "Blowing us back on our asses and then creeping off like a fuckin' pussy. Now all you got's a box of beer, and after we stick the shit out of you, we're gonna drink it all and then piss in your ear holes."

"Yeah, well — sorry about that." Earl pandered. "I just couldn't wait to show off these new fireworks that only explode in the direction you throw them." Roach cocked his head sideways, clenching his brow in befuddlement. Earl pounded his beer, reached into the box and grabbed another one, letting the rest of the 12 pack fall to the ground in front of his feet. "Look man, I know you guys are mad and I deserve to get stomped — please just let me have one more beer so it doesn't hurt so bad."

He cracked it and started chugging before they could answer. As he sucked down the suds he inhaled through his nose. The Derelicts approached Earl, the glint of steel protruding from their gloved hands and the damp desire for violence seeping from their mouths. The hatred for his enemies mixed in his guts with the alcohol, oxygen and carbonation — fusing into a toxic pocket of power that erupted from his esophagus like a sopping typhoon into the faces of his two would-be assailants. It sounded like a 10-foot-tall bullet train blasting out of a concrete tunnel with only nine-and-a-half feet of clearance and it smelled like the aftermath of a keg party in a salami factory.

As if slapped by a large invisible hand, the Derelicts each flew back ten feet and landed limp — knocked unconscious by the blast.

Earl stepped forward, wiping the drool and bile from his chin. A wave of shock swept over him — washing away his denial and replacing it with a jarring case of eye-popping clarity. After a few deep breaths he stepped backwards, turned and made a beeline for a cluster of trees at the far side of the park. "Hey kid, don't forget your beers," a voice growled. Earl skid to a halt and followed the voice over to the slide and monkey bars that were anchored to the swing set. He saw the silhouette of someone in a wide-brimmed cowboy hat and a trench coat.

"How long you been standing there?"

The gravelly voice of Pablo Vasquez echoed through the park. "Long enough to need a beer."

Chapter Seven

It's Time We Talked

Earl peered through the dim light of his apartment into the deep-set eyes of a haggard-looking puzzle. "Why are you following me?" he asked Pablo.

Pablo leaned forward in one of the two chairs Earl owned and exhaled a blue cloud of weed smoke. "Wrong question. The main issue here, is what took you so fucking long?"

"I don't know."

"Wong again!" Pablo snapped. "Those three words are the most disarming phrase in the whole motherfucking English language." He growled, removed his hat and started squeezing his temples between his right thumb and forefinger. "It's like W.C. Fields once said, 'If you can't dazzle them with brilliance, baffle them with bullshit.'" He stood up and began to pace as he ranted. "Admitting that you don't know immediately gives the other asshole the upper hand to do with you whatever the fuck he wants. If you don't know, don't just stand there like a bull with a bastard calf ... make something up! Lie your ass off or better yet, belch."

"I don't … ahem … I mean, well … I just kinda found out about this belching thing."

"I've heard about people like you, and after all the crazy shit I've seen I never doubted that sonic belch blasts were possible but seeing them up close ... man ... hot damn!" His laughter spread in warm gusts that seemed to momentarily dip in pitch.

"Speaking of weird shit …" Earl was getting brave. "You've got some explaining of your own to do. What was that weed smoking hypnosis stunt you pulled in the library the other day? While I was *working* no less."

"Alright you fuckin' dipshit." He cracked one of Earl's beers. "Listen close cuz the thin slice of salami stuck to your eyeballs is about to get peeled back permanently. There's a phenomenon at work in this biological construct we inhabit. Most people chalk it up to superstition but there's a name for what people like you and I deal with: Biomotive Anomalic Neurochemical Emanations. Yeah, I know — the acronym is a sick goddamn joke but there's accidental truth in it. It's literally the "BANE" of our existence. Most of the time, at least."

Earl cracked another beer, took a pull and gulped hard.

"Here's how it breaks down with me: my brain's pineal and pituitary glands overreact when I get really sad or pissed off or when I care too much or dare to give a shit. They release massive amounts of dopamine, serotonin, adrenaline, cortisol and epinephrine into my bloodstream. That chemical cocktail bonds with the THC in the weed I smoke to form a unique and powerful compound that then is catalyzed into action through my words. The molecular toxin secreted from the cells in my throat and mouth is highly mobile, and easily travels on the smoke exhalations that carry my emotionally charged mutterings. The result is that anyone in an ear or nostril shot temporarily experiences what doctors call Dysanachronometria — short term blackout with loss of motor functions."

"How did you find this out?"

"I smoke a lot of weed and I have a library card that I put to regular use."

Earl allowed himself a reluctant laugh. The first in a long time. "Heh ... hah ... ha ha ha bluuup," A gust of guttural wind whisked Pablo's beer from his hand and slammed it against the wall above his head just as he was taking a swig.

"Speaking of explanations, let's talk about you, kid."

"I'm all ears."

"I reckon that a life of suppressing your own voice has forced you to develop an unusually strong larynx, a really tough pharynx and fortified esophageal muscles. When you get pissed off or stressed out, agitated or otherwise excited your brain releases hormones into your bloodstream that react with the gas and alcohol accumulating in your stomach from all the beer. This reaction forms an energy pocket at the base of your gullet that is compounded by trapped emotions like passion, hate, love and fear. The resulting explosion whips through your vocal folds along with all the wind in your lungs making sonic wave blasts of a freakishly powerful sort."

"Huh?" Earl needed a minute. "So that's why the powerful sonic belching doesn't work with soda pop, eh? The reaction needs alcohol to catalyze?"

"Apparently so, but the chemistry of your abilities don't matter as much as the potential they hold. The issue is: how are you gonna put them to good use? You've put down the Derelicts twice now but as far as I'm concerned those guys are pissants compared to the forces at work out there that intend to shut people like you and me up for good."

"What forces?" Earl crossed his arms. "Shut people like us up why? What have *we* done?"

"The simple act of exercising our right to voice an opinion, in the ears of the elite few, is a threat to their power. You are finding your voice just in the nick of time. Any longer and you may have stayed silent forever. Lemme give you some advice, kid. Never go out without a few beers in your pocket, and if you can, always save one for later."

Chapter Eight

A Teacher's Gift

The next night, Pablo knocked on Earl's door holding an 18 pack of beer.

"I got something special for ya, kid."

"Yeah? Well, I'm kind of hungover. I thought I'd take it easy for once."

"Tough shit, twinkle toes," Pablo barked. "Take it easy my ass. There's no time for that. We gotta get you in shape. Build up your tolerance and hone your skills. You can't go out there like this. There's a world of dangerous motherfuckers out there, and most of them are smarter and deadlier than the Derelicts."

"So what?"

"So, let's drink!" Pablo hefted the box of beer and plopped it onto the coffee table with a *"whunk."*

Earl looked at the lettering on the side of the box, then reached in and pulled out a can. "What the fuck is this shit?"

He whined.

"For a guy who works in a library you sure are one illiterate bastard."

"I can read it, I've just never heard of it before. *Quasimodo Gold* ... really? Wow. Someone was dumb enough to name a beer after a piece of literature. No wonder I've never heard of it."

"Quit your bellyaching and crack one while it's still early. We've got work to do and if my hunch is correct, the high alcohol content in this shit is gonna give you a little something extra, ya know? It's 33% alcohol by volume and brewed in Gills Rock, Wisconsin — the last outpost on the peninsula that separates Lake Michigan from Green Bay. They say the winter wind out there is so damn strong and bitter cold it makes folks have visual and auditory hallucinations. Hence the name. They set this shit out to freeze a couple times during the fermentation period — makes it extra nasty."

Earl read the tagline on side of the can *"So Bitter You Can Hear It."* He took a pull and just about gagged. "Holy hell, man ... this stuff tastes like instant coffee spiked with turpentine."

"C'mon kid don't be a fucking pussy. Guzzle that shit back like a man."

After choking down three Quasimodo Golds, Earl finally asked, "Well, ain't you gonna drink one too?"

"Are you fucking kidding me? I wouldn't puke that shit up with your mama's mouth."

Earl finished the beer, crushed the can in his hand and said meekly, "Uhhh ... I think I'm almost ready."

Pablo reached into the 18 pack, "Here, take some of these for the road ... we're going for walk."

Two minutes later they stepped out onto the street in front of Earl's apartment building.

Chapter Nine

A Blur to a Focus

"OK kid" Pablo began. "Right now, you're like a sawed-off shotgun with a wide pattern spread — effective but only at a close distance. What we need to do is calibrate your aim and focus so that you can disable specific targets without hurting innocent bystanders."

"Yeah, I agree," Earl mumbled. "That's one of the reasons why this freaks me out. There's enough people getting hurt around here without me making things worse."

"Don't worry, we're gonna fix that. Now crack yourself a beer and slug it down."

"What? Out here on the street? If a cop drives by and sees me walking down the street drinking beer, he's gonna be up in my face in no time flat."

"I'll worry about that," Growled Pablo as he rolled a large joint, spilling not the tiniest of marijuana bits.

Earl opened a can of *Quasimodo Gold* and began sucking down the suds as they walked along 7th Avenue towards

Logan Street. Denver was quickly becoming a police state, with rollers lurking around every nighttime corner just itching to snag their hooks into anyone who looked remotely footloose. Earl was finishing off the beer as they crossed the alley entrance, and like clockwork, a police cruiser cast blinding beams in their direction as the car pulled to a stop 20 feet from Pablo and Earl.

Both front doors opened as Pablo lit his joint and inhaled. "You two," Barked the cop "Hands in the air, NOW!"

"Put out the cigarette, asshole," yelled the other cop

Pablo lifted both hands, leaving the joint in his mouth. He inhaled again and began chanting in a measured exhalation.

"This isn't your hour, and this isn't a cig,
here you have no power you stupid-ass pigs."

He blew a massive cloud of pot smoke into the cops' faces in a mighty gust. They both froze, the driver was reaching for his gun and the passenger side cop was interrupted just before barking another order.

"Ok kid. Quick now, crack another beer and take a pull.

"Hey man this looks really bad. We should get the hell out of here."

"Goddammit you fucking sissy, stop your lip and take a sip." Earl tipped the can and gulped hard.

"All right now, I want you to aim for the driver cop's hat. Just the hat. Don't blast all of him with a careless belch or you might cut him in half with the squad car door."

Earl inhaled and swallowed, focusing on the shiny brass badge in the center of the cop's hat. "Blaaap," he belched, throwing the cop backwards. The slamming car door barely missed his legs and the window shattered on impact.

"Dammit, you sloppy motherfucker," cursed Pablo. "Stop fucking around and try again on the other guy." Earl took another slug and readjusted, focusing again on the hat's badge and trying not to laugh at the cop's frozen expression that looked somewhere between confusion and severe indigestion.

Earl imagined an invisible fist smelling like beer and stomach bile flying from his mouth and he pushed it out "Boooiipp." The cop's hat zipped off his head, flew backwards and then rose vertically, riding on an updraft and landing on an adjacent grocery store roof.

"Nice one kid! Now let's get the fuck out of here before you get us in trouble with these shenanigans. Ain't your daddy ever taught you not to fuck with the cops?"

They scrambled down the street in a torrent of laughter and sloshing beer just as passersby were stopping to ponder the scene as both cops came to … struggling to comprehend what had taken place.

Several minutes later Earl and Pablo crouched amid the shadows in Sunken Gardens park. "Not bad for a beginner but remember, that was the equivalent of me holding the guy's arms from behind him while you slug him in the face."

Earl was still breathing heavily from the rush, "Not exactly fair, but man that felt good. I don't like cops."

"Nobody likes cops, not even other cops. They are universally resented and for a damn good reason. Most of them — not all of them — but most of them abuse their power, lie on police reports to cover their asses and confiscate illicit substances for their own purposes. Although nobody likes a lying bully who's a dope thief, assholes like that are not the main problem. On the scrotum pole of authority those guys are just the taint."

"Oh yeah," Earl joked, "who are the cock and balls, then?"

"Now you're starting to get it." Pablo nudged Earl, motioning for him to open another beer. "The Environmental Agency of Restrictions is the head of a heinous organization with bugs planted across the city and spies in every sub-segment of society. You've seen those ominous E.A.R. vans tooling around at all hours of the day and night, right? The ones with the question mark flanked by three parentheses on either side?"

"Yeah."

"Well, their job is to snoop around for anyone exercising their First Amendment rights with any sort of zest by playing loud music in a club, speaking out in public, playing tunes in their car, busking on the corner or even singing while walking down the street. These people get issued tickets called "Administrative Citations" to the tune of anywhere between $250.00 and $2,000.00. The money from the suckers who pay goes to fund the Agency and the poor fuckers who can't pay — they get hauled away by the cops who are simply instructed to follow all orders from EAR."

"Bluuup," Earl absentmindedly belched, sending Pablo's cowboy hat flying.

"Atta boy … much better!" Pablo said as he got up to fetch his Stetson.

Chapter 10

A Stench from Below

Deep in the bowels of the apartment building Earl called home, Luther Fisk was preparing a concoction of putrid proportions. He was muttering to himself as he worked. "I'm going to make them so sick they puke up their own shit."

The place was less of a dwelling and more of a forgotten basement storage room, unfit to house an average human but perfect for the most fragrant maintenance man in Denver. The walls were bare concrete — lined with rakes, shovels, hoses, and two worktables. One was mounted with a vice and a manual key-making machine, the other held a hot plate and an assortment of kitchen appliances salvaged from the apartment dumpsters. A mattress sat in one corner – atop it was a tepid nest of fabrics and hues; an old sleeping bag, a set of once-white sheets that were irreversibly stained dark brown and two pillows curled crisp with decades of dried drool. His squalor was not without amenities, he had a dorm-room sized refrigerator for what little food he acquired that he did not want to rot. Daily doses of cable TV hacked from an upstairs unit and broadcast across a cracked screen helped reinforce his disdain for humanity. He was rich with other people's trash, flourishing in a musty palace adorned with the treasures of reimagined rubbish.

He opened a quart of milk and poured chunks of fermenting curds and decomposing whey into a blender caked with dried brown slime. He added two cups of prune juice, a glop of beans crawling with maggots, a raw green apple, three broccoli twigs, seven brussels sprouts, a handful of asparagus chutes and five wriggling cockroaches. He then slapped on the lid and hit the *"puree"* button. As he watched the medley whir into a green blur, the ferocity of the blender blades chopping through vegetable matter, bugs and bits of congealed cow juice made him dizzy with anticipation. He had resolve, however, and he left it out to fester overnight and went to bed hungry. He dreamed of saturated urinal cakes sprinkled with rat turds and served with a side of drain grime.

Around 9:00 AM the next morning, he gulped down the rancid blender sludge in one famished backwards lurch. As he sat down to work on some knitting, his guts groaned in approval after finally being fed, then gurgled as they set to work sorting it all out, breaking down the already decaying matter and systematically turning it into methane.

Three hours later, he sauntered into Bank of the Republic on the 100 block of South Broadway wearing a knitted pink ski mask, a green t-shirt, a pair of dirty grey sweatpants with a mustard stain across the crotch and a drab green Army-issue rucksack. A rotund security guard advanced quickly to intercept him. "Hold it right there mister, you can't walk into a bank with a mask over your face!"

"What do you think, I'm here to rob the place? I mean, clearly you can see that I have no weapons. My face is cold, that's all."

"OK wise guy. I'm going to have to ask you to leave."

"Tsk tsk," Luther taunted, waving his right index finger back and forth in front of the guard's face, a fresh booger was wedged beneath his black nail and draped over to one side. Luther feinted as though he meant to leave. "So quick to judge," he sighed. "Your discrimination, I'm afraid, is making me fume with spite."

He turned around and bent over, his butt mere inches from the security guard's midsection, and he released a gastric explosion forming a green cloudburst that quickly shot through every cubic inch of the lobby. It sounded like a cardboard box being ripped open in a Wyoming headwind. It smelled like a maggot-ridden skunk carcass smeared across the highway on a balmy summer afternoon. The guard was lifted off his feet by the blast and began vomiting even before his ass hit the floor fifteen feet away. As he landed the sound of two dozen other limp bodies slapping onto the marble floor bounced off the walls in a din that sounded like a round of applause. The fibers in his mask protected him from his own stench as he stepped over passed out customers, making his way to the nearest teller's window.

He stood over a woman's limp body that was slumped to the side in a chair. "Ok missy, I'm going to need you to stop sleeping on the job and open these drawers for me." He withdrew a smelling salt packet from his rucksack and broke it open under her nose. A jet of ammonia gas shot up her nostrils and jolted her awake.

"Whuuuuuh! What the hell is going on?"

"You're being robbed, you stupid bitch. Now open these drawers and you won't get hurt."

When the Gasser's vapor struck, the bank teller was lucky enough to have passed out upright, saving the seven-month-old fetus in her womb from harm. He noted her distended midsection, her long, shapely legs and her round bosom — no doubt swollen from gestation. As she sat up, she brushed the brown hair out of her eyes and pleaded. "Please don't hurt me. I'm going to have a baby soon."

"Listen sweetie pie, if you don't unlock these cash drawers for me RIGHT NOW — I am going to shove my fist up your snatch, yank that little bundle of joy straight from your cunt and beat you to death with the little brat. Got it?"

She cooperated with haste and the Gasser quickly emptied all five teller drawers. Two minutes later, Luther Fisk strolled from the front doors of the Bank of the Republic, mask still intact, and bolted across Broadway. He disappeared into the Baker district like an ape running into the jungle. His tarnished garb and whimsical hat were ample camouflage, as was his tattered backpack that happened to contain upwards of $25,000.00.

Chapter 11

Method Belching

"OK kid, you're doing pretty all right so far but you're gonna have to step things up a notch if you want to be of any goddamn use at all."

"Jesus Pablo, what the hell are you talking about now? I'm still hungover from all that *Quasimodo Gold.*"

Pablo had walked Earl home the night before, and barely gave him six hours of sleep before rattling him awake and continuing his tutelage. He had let himself back in and was now standing over Earl as he struggled up from the crusty embrace of the couch.

"Sit up straight, Waldo. If you want to belch for the greater good, you're gonna need to hone your skill. You gotta learn how to summon your power even when your emotions are numbed by all the beer."

"Huh?"

"All fights in the real world are on a two-way street. You possess a unique ability — one of staggering potential. In order to utilize it, though, you gotta become disabled to a certain degree by the fact that you need beer to harness your power. This means you're gonna have to learn how to better handle your hooch and to utilize 'the method.'"

"The method?"

"If you were a theater geek or gave a shit about culture, you'd know what I mean you goddamn luddite. It's OK, I'll spare you the lecture and get to the point. The basic gist of the situation is that booze numbs your emotions, which are key to the dimensional magnitude of your belching prowess. You need to be able to access your deepest passions, fears, motivations and hatreds while you're half in the bag."

"How the fuck am I supposed to do that?"

Pablo held out his empty right hand, "The answer is right here."

"There ain't nothing there."

"Take a closer peek. C'mon son, look real good now."

Earl leaned in closer to Pablo's hand. As he squinted, Pablo's left palm came whizzing in from Earl's periphery and slapped him hard across the right side of his face with a loud "*WHAP*."

"Owww you sonofabitch! What the fuck did you do that for?" Earl was instantly furious. He rubbed his face and dared to think about hitting back.

"You feel that sting, kid? You notice how the adrenalin shoots into your veins in a nanosecond and — even though I'm your friend — you instinctively want to bust my jaw?"

"Yeah, asshole. I noticed."

"Good. You're going to have to memorize that immediate surge of emotion. To become so intimate with it that you can conjure it up from the depths of your subconscious at will — like a psychic cyclone — and harness it for belching magnitude. Your talents are useless unless applied with raw feelings. With passion and pain. With lust and rage. With courage and fury. With fear and sadness. With disgust. With trust. With joy. With love."

Pablo's deep-set brown eyes were like lasers burning holes into Earl's corneas, through his brain hemispheres and into the bone on the inside of the back of his skull. The dope smoking poet in the cowboy hat was either the world's most intense liar or one sincerely impassioned Soothsayer.

"This is just the beginning, son. You can't live apart from yourself anymore. You've got to open the valve to your humanity like pulling the tap handle on a keg of beer. Your leverage is thirst for justice."

Chapter 12

I Spit in Your Face

Cricket waited outside the History Colorado Museum on South Broadway between 12th and 13th Avenues. Her jet-black hair fanned out in a jagged drape over the wide collar of her full-length black overcoat. The front was open, revealing a black turtleneck top tucked into ebony leather pants rolled up over well-worn combat boots. The skin-tight fit around her legs revealed the riveting curvature of calves, thighs and buttocks sculpted by frequent exercise. Her torso was supple yet firm, two Venus de Milo-like breasts perched atop a washboard abdominal core.

Her silver flask glinted beneath the streetlights as she drew it from her inside jacket pocket and considered the contents. The autumn drizzle was turning into a light snowfall that practically mandated drinking to stave off the impending freeze. She screwed off the cap and snuck a nip of tequila blanco just after an EAR van went whizzing by. A crowd of political fundraiser attendees were dispersing from the museum. She picked a well-dressed middle-aged couple advancing towards the curb to meet their driver. They looked like two sticks of vanilla-flavored saltwater taffy fresh off the assembly line. Cricket pulled out a cigarette and lipped it, "Hey bitch, do you or that sack of shit you're bilking for all he's worth have a light?"

"Sweet lord," the woman gasped, "please watch your language."

"Oh now, Gloria," the man pandered. "I'm sure we can find something for the little wretch."

"Well aren't you sweet, Walter."

As he reached towards his back pocket, she lifted the flask to her lips again and swigged a mouthful, swished it around violently and then shuddered. Instead of a wallet, Walter pulled out a stun gun with his right hand and zapped it a few times in anticipation. The light from the blue arc between the electric prongs glinted off Cricket's shimmering overcoat. He lurched forward, trying to thrust 80,000 volts of electricity into her body. She slipped to her left side like a matador and spewed a jet of saliva-spiked agave with quickly catalyzing neurotoxins into his eyes. Gloria reached for her pepper spray and received a stinging gush of the same.

"Oh god damn the little bitch blinded me!" Walter screamed.

"Aaaaauuuuggghhh someone help me!" Gloria squawked. "I just got stabbed in the eyes!"

Wiry hands in black leather gloves quickly rifled through Walter's pockets as he wailed and flailed. Cricket darted about him like a mongoose, deftly avoiding the miniature lightning still zapping in his hand. Her now-sightless victim was determined to exact justice.

Gloria was floundering about, desperately grasping at the air for Walter and wailing. Blinded as well, Walter groped at the air around him and his hand found the wrong wrist. "I got you, you thieving little cunt!" He held it tight, guesstimating where the arm owner's torso would most likely be and thrust the stun gun outward. The prongs of the stun gun dug into the supple tissue of Gloria's right breast. Her arms involuntarily shot outward and her hand muscles clenched, causing her thumb to dispense a hissing stream of pepper spray into Walter's eyes. Her body went limp and crumpled onto the sidewalk like a ragdoll while Walter fell backwards onto his ass in awe, embarrassment, agony and blubbering disbelief — which made Cricket's job of stealing the rest of their valuables all the easier.

They were relieved of one leather wallet, a pearl necklace, a gold wristwatch, a silver brooch, an abundant money clip and two diamond-dazzled wedding rings. Realizing what he had done, the man sobbed next to his wife, "Oh darling, please forgive me."

Cricket stole off into the night, feeling not the slightest twinge of remorse. These people were entitled — she was a have not. Yet, she was determined by a self-sworn pledge to not have nothing.

Gloria came to a few minutes later and sobbed, "Why did you call me a cunt and then zap me? You are a stupid, clumsy, retarded, bastard!"

An hour later a demoralized Walter recounted their debacle to a Denver Police Department detective. Gloria stewed next to him, trembling and muttering under her breath. "I got you, you thieving little cunt?" she asked. "You thieving little cunt?"

"There had to have been at least three of them, maybe four," Walter explained to the cop. "Thankfully, I was able to get the stun gun away, but not after they shocked my poor wife here."

Gloria seethed. "You're an idiot. A complete fucking moron."

Chapter 13

Knockers

After the initial guidance from The Soothsayer, Earl realized he needed to strike out on his own. Pablo's instructional visits were becoming less frequent, and it was clear that the next chapter in his belching education was to be self-taught.

He thought about his years of cowardice — of standing quietly by while entitled assholes stomped, snatched, burned, raped and murdered with little or no recourse. He had witnessed countless carjackings and purse snatchings. While he wanted to help, he never knew how. All he could do was keep his head down and shuffle out of the way or stand there and wait to be next.

Earl didn't have to go far to find trouble. He lived just a few blocks west of Broadway in the Baker District. All he had to do was head over to Jackknife Liquors, pick up a 12 pack of beer and sometime during the errand the night would be pierced by the screams of someone being mugged.

One night after Pablo had been absent for a few days, Earl headed out for a nighttime stroll. Before placing the 12 pack of Quasimodo Gold into his backpack, he removed a can at the checkout counter and began chugging. "Ah ha! I see you thirsty again!" joked Kim. "Dlink up, muddafucka!" Earl said nothing, but as he turned to the door, he directd a dense, short belch at the handle that said PUSH. It flew open with a clamor of door chimes yet did not shatter. Progress.

As Earl stepped onto Broadway he turned right and headed north, making his way towards the Mayan Theater. He walked beneath the marquee finishing his third beer and then he heard the screams. "Somebody help me! I'm being attacked! Help me, please!" Across Broadway just before 4th, Earl saw several figures struggling at the RTD bus stop. He tore across the street, his remaining nine cans of Quasimodo Gold knocking about in his backpack. As he approached, he saw one guy pointing a knife at a woman's face while another attempted to yank her purse from her clutches and a third guy stood by wringing his hands with excitement and shifting his weight from one foot to another. "Shut the fuck up bitch and let it go or homeboy here is gonna slice up that pretty face of yours!"

"Hey assholes," Earl shouted and then inhaled deeply. "Step away from her. Now."

The knife wielder looked over at Earl "Oh yeah motherfucker? What you got, huh?" He took a step at Earl, the blade glinted in the moonlight and the desperation of addiction quivered in the man's eyeballs.

"BLUUUUUP" Earl's belch lifted the man up and slammed his head through the plexiglass wall of the bus stop shelter. His body went limp and he hung there like a ragdoll. The hand wringer made a screech and lunged forth, looking to get his wiry mitts around Earl's neck but Earl had another belch queued up and with a violent "*BLAAAP*" he sent the second man's head through the glass right next to his partner. As the body went limp, Earl heard a loud *"rrrrriiip"* as he was summoning up another belch to deal with the third guy, who suddenly froze in place with his mouth agape. He had ripped open the woman's blouse and revealed the largest set of breasts Earl had ever seen, held firmly into place by a lacy pink brassiere. The guy was mesmerized, stupefied in fact. She reached into her purse, pulled out a set of brass knuckles and with a deft right hook to the temple sent the third assailant to the ground. He landed with the unmistakable sound of a human face hitting concrete — like a cantaloupe being hurled against a brick wall. Sirens snapped Earl out of the trance washing over him. "Come on dude!" the woman snapped. "They're gonna nail your ass for assaulting these fuckheads! Follow me!"

She tore down 4th, one hand clenching her torn lapels together and the other holding the purse she had never let go of. Earl was close behind her, and as they hung a right onto Acoma Street, he looked over his shoulder to see a cop car and two EAR vans come skidding up to the crime scene.

Two minutes later they crouched in a basement apartment with the lights off. Flashlights scanned across the garden level windows as the authorities searched for them. "Stay quiet," a female voice whispered. "Don't fucking move." The two strangers waited in silence until Earl detected movement, and then a lamp clicked on. "My name is Elsa," she said with a smile. "Who the fuck are you?"

The warm interior light revealed a curvaceous woman in her mid-thirties with hips like the exaggerated cutaway of a Dobro guitar. Her skin seemed to glow, and despite pockmarks from a presumably troubled past she was captivating — like a troubled Sophia Vergara look-alike who just wandered in from a hailstorm. Behind her was a tapestry of velvet curtains, long strings of glittering beads and shelves crammed with knickknacks, books, and candles. The air was thick with the aroma of vanilla and another scent he couldn't quite make out. "Well … are you just gonna sit there or are you going to offer me a goddamn beer?"

Earl pulled a beer out of his backpack and opened it. It foamed over from all his recent running but before he could slurp up the suds Elsa snatched it from him and placed her crimson lips over the can opening and sucked in hard. He was determined not to stammer as he attempted to engage in the conversation. "I'm Earl. I heard you screaming, and I wanted to help."

"Thanks, dude. I can usually handle myself, but those motherfuckers are strung out and desperate. They snuck up on me and I couldn't get my defense together fast enough. You know, lately I've heard some rumors about someone like you going around fucking things up — but with all the shit talking lunatics in this city I figured it was just another heap of nonsense."

"What have you heard?"

"I heard there was some nutjob going around with some kind of an air cannon mowing down gangsters and cops."

Earl cracked a beer for himself. "Hmmmm. Well, I suppose that's somewhat true. Did you know those guys who were trying to mug you?"

"Sort of. They were trying to hire me for a gang bang, but I don't fuck junkies." Earl took a hard swallow of his beer and looked down at the shag-carpeted floor.

"Come on, man deal with it. Don't act like you've never met a prostitute."

"Well, actually …"

"Holy sheeeeit! A crude motherfucker like you going around burping louder than a goddamn hot rod without a muffler and you've never bothered to mingle with hookers?"

"Well, I … uh …"

"Oh whatever, man. No biggie — I'm just messing with you. You know, you're not the only one with special talents." She let the two halves of her torn blouse fall to either side, her perfectly shaped breasts seemed to heave forward, threatening to burst from the pink lace and knock both of Earl's eyeballs back into his skull. He became entranced as all the blood rushed from his brain, down his torso and into his dick. He felt a singular magnetic urge drawing his consciousness straight into the captivating canyon of her magnificent cleavage. He felt himself falling forward when Elsa smacked him hard across the face and snapped him out of his trance.

"Why are people always slapping me?" He thought aloud.

"That's why they call me Knockers. Because men get hypnotized by my chest — somehow — and I can either knock them out with my brass knuckles and take their loot, slap them back into reality or give them the most enthralling, enchanting fuck of their lives. It depends on my mood and when my rent is due."

"Wow. I'm so sorry ... I didn't mean to stare. I just … I don't know. Something came over me."

"It's OK," Elsa explained. "Something about my biochemistry is off. The skin on my tits emits massive amounts of female pheromones and it just stops guys dead in their tracks. Be glad I didn't show you my nipples or you would have cum in your pants and passed the fuck out."

Earl took a pull from his beer and looked away and prayed for his hard-on to go down. "Yeah. Thanks for not doing that. I really appreciate it."

"No problem. Consider us even. Just one thing though — you don't tell anyone you met Knockers or that you know where I live, and I won't tell anyone I know what you look like. Which — by the way — isn't an 'Earl.' What's your street name?"

"My street name? I don't have one."

"Bullshit motherfucker … you do now. You're The Belcher."

Chapter 14

Toxic Anal Vapors

This was a bad time to be a pregnant woman in Denver — especially if you worked in a bank. The only thing Luther Fisk hated more than women and children was when they were both in the same body. Every day his fantasies became more explicit. He relished the idea of tying down a pregnant woman, reaching up inside of her and grabbing her unborn child around the neck. Then, he imagined he would taunt her as he yanked it from her womb and beat her to death with it. The only thing stopping him from realizing these daydreams was the fact that he was a one-man operation. Due to his poor diet and his sickly state of internal health, he was too weak to abduct a woman on his own.

Until recently, he was unaware that his fantasy was impossible unless a woman was in labor. He was studying charts of internal human anatomy, trying to figure out ways to maximize his putrid emissions by learning all he could about the human G.I. tract. One day he stumbled upon a cross section diagram of a pregnant woman. He realized that getting past the cervix was going to require more than just his bare hands. Regardless, the fact that his only influence over womankind was to repulse them because he stunk so

47

bad made him hate the mothers-to-be he encountered even more.

In addition to double homicide abortions, The Gasser also had a serious fascination with shit. The stench associated with human excrement was the very source of his power and he reveled in the fact that he had guts that could produce it with more gusto than anyone else in the world. He would fantasize aloud, "I'm going to gag them out so bad they shit themselves." He had become obsessed with the idea of producing a cloud of anal vapor so toxic that it triggered instantaneous diarrhea in anyone who breathed it in. His new and improved strategy of stench consisted of large chunks of garlic and cauliflower along with wads of cabbage and kale dipped in raw sewage (for lubrication) and swallowed whole. The longer the food sat in his guts being broken down, the more time methane gas had to form. The high content of hydrogen sulfide in sewage simply meant an additional fragrance of rotten eggs would be mixed into his emissions.

Being the maintenance man for a large apartment complex meant that Luther had access to the exterior plumbing cleanouts, past which the daily excrement of many residents flowed. It seemed that lately, however, someone in the building was drinking an awful lot of beer which wasn't all that bad.

The night he discovered this new delicacy, he had crept out into the alley out of curiosity and removed the iron cover to the sewer cleanout hole. Then, he dipped in a rusty ladle, lifted it to his lips and sipped at the sewage like a chef sampling the evening broth. "Exquisite," he smacked. "The faint hint of hops really takes the edge off."

Chapter 15

The Kindness of a Stranger

With a twelve pack of *Quasimodo Gold* in his backpack, Earl set out to confront the noxious man who was terrorizing Denver. Copies of *The Denver Post* were flying off the racks because of compelling headlines like "Gastric Terror Cripples Banks" and "Flatulent Bandit Strikes Again."

One October afternoon he wandered the streets, following a foul stench northeast from his place in Baker towards Capitol Hill. Anticipating an altercation, he systematically drank beers as he marched forth, hiding the cans within the cylinder of his black hoodie sleeve. He had rigged a system for discreet public guzzling by affixing a ¼ inch tube from within the right side of his hood, down the inside of his arm and to the hem of the wrist cuff. It was held in place by gaffer's tape, and the mouth end was mangled from nervous chewing. Blatantly sucking down beers in broad daylight was a bad idea and a good way to disappear into an EAR van. He had just tossed his fourth empty can into a dumpster and affixed a fresh one into his tube sleeve when he heard the faint sound of a muffled scream. He was at 14th and Emerson, stopped in front of the Parental Planninghood building. He noticed that the windows seemed to be fogging over with some sort of green mist. The air was rife with the stench of rotten eggs and sewage. He ran up to the building, yanked open the door and with a gag of gastronomic girth he dissolved the foul cloud. "BLLLUUUUUUUUUPP!" He looked around to see the writhing bodies of a receptionist, a nurse and several others strewn about the floor and moaning.

The screams were clearer now, "Someone help! I'm suff ...o ... ca ..."A woman's voice trailed off and was followed by a "thud" from just beyond the reception room wall. He burst into an adjoining exam room, beer in hand. Through the green fog he could see the figure of someone in a trench coat crouching over a limp body sprawled across the exam table. It was his old nemesis from the elevator ripping away the panties of an unconscious pregnant woman with one hand and clawing at her crotch with the other. "I'm gonna rip that little brat straight outta your snatch and beat you to death with it!" he snarled.

Earl tossed his head back, squeezed an entire can of beer into his mouth — jettisoning the froth straight down his throat. He swallowed hard and took aim "BLLLARARARARARRRRPPP." His belch sounded like a crosscut saw being banged back and forth between two tree trunks. He was able to direct his sonic blast at the Gasser's body without hitting the woman. Surprised by the barrage, Luther turned towards Earl just in time to be slammed sideways into the wall and knocked unconscious. As he slid to the floor the outline of his body was indented into the drywall.

Earl scooped up the woman and carried her into the reception room where the others were beginning to wake up. He gently set her down onto one of the benches realizing at this point it would be nice to know CPR. He leaned towards her mouth, put his lips upon hers and belched a tiny yet powerful gust of inflation into her lungs. She took a deep breath, and her eyelids began to flutter. "Oh God. Stinks so bad. Please make sure my baby is ok." The nurse shoved Earl aside, took the girl's pulse and checked her pupils.

As Earl stood up and turned towards the door a familiar skunk-faced figure burst from the exam room bleeding from the left side of his head. "Hey shitmouth!" he barked. Earl turned toward the voice just as The Gasser flung a handful of brownish-green goo at his face. He ducked and a putrid wad of fresh crap whizzed past his head and hit the front window with a splat. Luther used the diversion to prance past Earl and the stunned staff of Parental Planninghood. He sprung from the front door into the 30-degree autumn air, cut right onto 14th Avenue and sprinted west. Earl was close behind, pulling a fresh beer from his backpack, cracking it open and gulping it down as he ran.

Luther hung a right onto Clarkson and then veered left into the massive parking lot of Astronaut Liquors. Earl faced him down between two rows of parked cars. The Gasser began clawing at his own abdomen, activating his gastric juice to conjure up some chemical artillery. Earl was doing the same, only his hand clawed at the inside of his backpack, grasping his last two cans of Quasimodo Gold. Pablo's advice echoed in his head, "Always save one for later."

"Hello again shitmouth! It's a good thing you've got your little sippy sippy with you, you're gonna need it to wash this down." The Gasser turned around, looking over his right shoulder, flipping his trench coat around his left hip and exposing but a thin layer of filthy cotton cloth between his asshole and the open air. Earl knew what was coming and sucked back some more of his beer and inhaled. Simultaneous explosions boomed, one from the Gasser in a steaming green cloud of rancid gas — the other from Earl's gullet in a frothy gust of guttural rage. The two storm fronts met like high- and low-pressure systems, forming a whirling dervish — a momentary funnel that whipped up the wind velocity of a F2 tornado and washed the entire block in a stench of bile-basted hops and piss-pickled lutefisk. The circular gust knocked them both backwards, rolling Luther end over end like a spare tire and Earl sideways like an empty keg.

Sirens pierced the air as Luther gathered himself and scurried across Colfax Avenue into the shadows of the Uptown District. Earl expected cop cars but was surprised to see two ominous black Environmental Agency of Restrictions vans advancing toward him from Washington Street. They both had air horns and flashing lights but were devoid of the "*To Serve and Protect*" motto, which somehow made them slightly more respectable than the average law enforcement vehicle. The lead van was equipped with high-powered speakers above each front seat window that blared at him, "Do not move. You are under arrest for detonation of explosive devices within the city limits and disturbing the peace." Perched atop the rear van sat a curious black disc-like object that reminded Earl of a super-oversized hockey puck. He could hear Pablo's voice in his head again, 'Well c'mon kid. Don't just stand there with your thumb in your ass, do something." He still had a couple of gulps in his second-to-last can of beer.

The lead EAR van advanced across the parking lot until it was halfway between Washington and Clarkson Streets. A crowd of gawkers had gathered outside Astronaut Liquors. Most were yuppies and Capitol Hill hipsters peppered with the typical ragamuffin hustlers and the occasional-if-not-rare drop-dead gorgeous dame. The van then veered to the right at a 45-degree angle, revealing the rear vehicle. They both came to a stop and the loudspeaker blared at Earl again, "Now, very slowly put the detonator down, turn around and place your hands on your head."

"It's not a detonator, asswipe ... it's a fucking beer!" He very slowly brought the can up to his face. He could hear the sliding door on the passenger side of the van thrust open and the hard soles of combat boots stomping onto the pavement. The navy-blue EAR infantry jumpsuits and matching military-style fitted caps made them look like a squad of flight school dropouts.

The loudspeaker blared again, "Put the detonator down, or you will be fired upon."

"You want me to put this down? OK, down the hatch." He tossed his head back and sucked down the rest of the beer, letting the can fall from his right hand and roll away. As half a dozen M-16 barrels took aim at him he belched forth a booming blast that thrust like a giant fist into the EAR squad, tossing each man backwards 10 feet and slamming the EAR van into a row of parked cars. Glass shattered, steel crunched, car alarms screeched, onlookers screamed and the loudspeaker issued an order of another sort. "Hit him with The Puck. Slapshot this asshole, now!"

The black disc atop the second van shot a sound bullet, an invisible cannonball, an intense pulse of megahertz that hit Earl in in the midsection and knocked him back several yards. It knocked the wind out of him temporarily, and he rolled over onto his stomach slowly pulling his knees up beneath him. He remained hunched over, struggling to regain his breath and fumbling through his backpack for the last can of Quasimodo Gold. He had quickly gone from frightened to extremely pissed off. As soon as he cracked the top of the beer can he jammed the straw-end in his sleeve into the hole

53

and sucked the contents down through the straw-end in his hood while gasping to refill his lungs. "Lay down flat and put your hands behind your head." The loudspeaker decibels had been increased and were rolling over him in deafening waves. As he stood up the order was given, "Slapshot him again, full power." He dropped to his belly and rolled to his left as the sound bullet from The Puck whizzed past his head and decimated the rear-view window of a green Hummer.

The crowd's curiosity turned to panic as people began running back into Astronaut Liquors for cover — except for the silhouette of one figure, which advanced forward with slow, steady steps and was obscured by the backlighting of the storefront neons. Earl turned and focused on the center of the puck as he inhaled his first full breath and belched out a furious guttural gust. The Puck fired at the same time and both sonic bullets barely missed one another, as the warping air about them threw each off course. Instead of in the midsection Earl was hit in the shins, knocking him over, nonetheless. The top end of The Puck was bent backwards, and the two EAR agents operating it were knocked off the van and onto the concrete. "Hit him again, goddammit, and stop fucking around," the loudspeaker was angry as well.

"Sir," a shaky voice said outside of Earl's earshot. "The Puck is inoperable."

The loudspeaker answered, "OK forget it you fucking idiots. Just run his ass over, will you?"

Earl was out of beer and he couldn't feel his feet. He was struggling to stand up but could not maintain his balance. He heard every ounce of horsepower in the EAR van engine rev to attention. He knelt there before it, crippled and separated by nothing but a couple dozen yards. A shadow moved next to him between two parked cars and as he turned his head,

Cricket emerged from her cover clutching a large Astronaut Liquors bag. "You wouldn't happen to have any beer in there, would you" Earl gasped.

"As a matter of fact, I do, but you're gonna owe me one," she quipped as she tossed him a can. He caught it and cracked it fast.

"Get the fuck out of here, now!" He yelled before jamming the can into his face and crushing it — forcing the beer down his throat in a fast-frothy stream.

The EAR van was gaining speed and was within 50 feet of splattering Earl's guts across the parking lot. Rather than retreating, Cricket just crouched there, a mere two feet from Earl and watched with utter fascination. They were both about to be pummeled into flesh and bone goop when Earl aimed a belch at the base of the speeding van's grill — now just 10 feet away — which lifted it up over their heads and sent it crashing into a silver Mercedes Benz SL-Class, a bright orange Jeep Rubicon and a white Cadillac Escalade. "Gimme another beer, fast!" Cricket tossed him a can and as he swallowed yellow carbonated magic, he noticed familiar words on the label. *Quasimodo Gold*. He belched another crippling blow to the first van and its occupants, who were advancing with confusion. "Hey! Where are you?" Cricket had disappeared after the second belch.

"I'm over here, hurry!" She was climbing through the passenger window of a blue Dodge Challenger. Earl crawled towards her military style. The door popped open and he pulled himself inside as the engine roared to life. She had hot-wired the car in a matter of seconds. They pulled from the Astronaut Liquors parking lot onto Clarkson Street as another EAR van and several police cars pulled in from the Washington Street entrance. The confusion and destruction served as ample cover, and they drove away undetected.

An exhausted, slack jawed, half-drunk Earl looked over at his savior. She kept her eyes on the road. "My name is Cricket."

"I'm Earl."

Chapter 16

Blatherskite

Raul Geisel locked the door to the inner sanctum of the top floor of the EAR Headquarters building. His political prowess and penchant for manipulation were bested only by his innate loathing for having to endure the opinions of others. It began as the unruly behavior of an only child with an overactive mouth, a vacuous yearning for attention and an apathetic audience. The simple tendency to throw a tantrum when adults were present in order to command their fixation developed into an unending need for validation. By the time he was a teenager, his unquenchable thirst for adoration led him to pursue theatre and music. But alas, since his only genuine emotion was contempt for others it was soon revealed that he was one extremely shitty artist. At least that's what he thought, until he discovered the art of manipulation. By his early twenties he had all but mastered the ability to gain the trust of others, discover their weaknesses and exploit them into servitude or annihilate them completely.

This ability was parlayed into a short, somewhat successful but ultimately humiliating career as a music promoter. Trading one matrix of ulterior motives, yes men and underhanded politics for another — Raul made a lateral move into civic duty. He began working for the City of Denver as a parking ticket dispenser and gradually advanced to an administrative position in the Department of Public Works. He eventually gained enough influence and leverage to propose the Environmental Agency of Restrictions, masquerading as a crusader against air and light pollution while secretly developing a plan to silence all forms of articulate acoustic expression and sonic beauty. He dreamed of a Denver frozen with fear — a city gripped by tiptoe paranoia. A rattled populace fixated on the fact that the slightest meaningful utterance could result in fines, harassment, arrest, detainment, incarceration and even execution. He dreamed of a city humming with inane chatter instead of eloquence, computer simulated noise instead of orchestrated instrumentation and baseless arguments in place of constructive conversation. All intermittently eclipsed by deafening sirens sent to pursue and apprehend those who dared audibly emote with any hint of emotional currency.

Although he was a lousy stage actor, through years of whipping layers of lies into filibustering tirades of bullshit he discovered he possessed a curious power. The more he carried on, the less personal will anyone listening to him seemed to retain. The more he blabbered about non sequitur nonsense, the weaker the listener became. With enough time and horseshit to jabber about, he could systematically coerce a rational person into following barbaric orders and agreeing with appalling ideas. It was a form of hypnosis that paid incredible dividends. Years of trapping colleagues and breaking them down with diatribes of mesmerizing drivel had given him the political leverage to not only traverse the pecking order but to climb over the backs of his superiors. Once broken, a colleague could be coerced into divulging their deepest secrets and ugliest transgressions. Recordings of these sessions played back to his victims made it easy to demand political favors, payoffs of hush money and criminal behavior unbecoming of those supposedly working in "public service."

There was one catch. Talking nonstop at certain cadence and decibel level with a ratio of diminishing logic versus increasing nonsense was exhausting. This was, however, the optimal mode of yammering that rendered the greatest results. So, to keep up with energetic demand, Raul invented a compound he lovingly referred to as MORE. Quite simply, it was an inhalable mixture of methamphetamine, OxyContin, Ritalin and Ecstasy. Amid his charade of deceit and lies there sat the one truth: if you snorted just a little of this shit — you'd always want more.

The podium on the EAR auditorium stage was painted bleach white with a black (((?))) symbol emblazoned across the width of the front. Standing behind it arms outstretched, Geisel would launch into a mind-numbing tirade that would systematically render weak-brained, video-game-addicted teens and young adults into obedient enactors of his will. His screed was intelligible to a degree, but essentially a mish-mash of social idealism, political rhetoric, cryptic allegory and pure gibberish. He would prepare for his rant by snorting a couple fat lines of MORE and taking a deep breath. He would then stretch his face back into a painful wince, as though he had a broken tailbone and he'd just been kicked in the nuts — then he would let the blather fly forth ...

"Interference is a sacrificial act selflessly performed in the interest of the greater good. Citizens are leaves on the branches of the tree of humanity. When left untrimmed these twigs can become wild menacing boughs with no regard for structures, fences and boundaries. When fighting for the greater good, arms are like branches that can be hacked off and used as weapons. It is a powerful act of immediate state-sponsored justice to beat a man to death with his own severed limb. As dead fists clench for the last time they may do so around your manhood but never up your backside. Fields of deadwood sing no operas neither at the dawn of the dribbling nor at the edge of the wipe. Bountiful belief broadens the sword that softens the brain with butter before splitting it in half. You must glint like a razor, descend like a pyramid and close like a door."

At this point, anyone within earshot who did not have the cerebral discipline to tune out such oblique yammering became piqued within its grip. The seduction was subtle, subliminal and complete. Geisel could literally bullshit an entire throng of people into compliance like a hypnotist comedian making bloated tourists behave like chickens. After running through his tirade twice, his subjects would begin to nod in time with his syllabic cadence. Entire squadrons of EAR recruits could be subjugated, hypnotized and systematically conditioned.

"Right is wrong noise is silence spite all song with boisterous violence. Opinions are lies to stifle and mute we minions are eyes with rifles we shoot.

Auditorium rows of previously unsuspecting cadets would coalesce in an en masse incantation — thundering like the footfalls of an advancing army.

"All lines must be straight all angles upright, the fine for curved paint is swift loss of sight. To laugh is to litter while dancing pollutes, we will turn them to quitters when we make them all mute."

The sensation of one hundred cadets chanting his inane mantras of social control gave him an incredible rush of self-aggrandizement. A temporary occupier of the massive void inside him no typical human interaction could provide. Like any addiction, every bolstering instance of brainwashing-induced allegiance needed to be followed by another of equal or preferably greater power. He was a junkie addicted to MORE and the blind subservience facilitated by its consumption.

To the uninitiated, these were nothing more than pep rallies with blustering chants, pumping up the troops for their impending foray into public service. Geisel, a master hypnotist, wasted no opportunities to embed his will deep into the mushy minds of his men with post-hypnotic reinforcement.

He ended every EAR agent orientation speech with a clearly-stated directive. "It's simple, people. Painting, music, poetry, dancing and anything that remotely resembles self-expression will not be tolerated. Free speech and independent thought are enemies of civilization and must be detected, sniffed out and squashed. Offenders will be detained, questioned, tortured, turned and farmed for information. We are going to turn Denver into a perfect city, organized, predictable, clean and controlled. It shall become the model for every other major metropolitan area in this country, on this continent, in this hemisphere and on this planet."

Geisel's recruits were selected because they showcased impressionable mental constitution upon first being interviewed. After just one orientation session with Blatherskite, the minds of most had been ground to a dull stump and were helplessly tethered to the will of EAR.

By the time The Belcher had emerged from the innards of Earl Danners, Blatherskite was zeroing in on his directive to circumvent the First Amendment. He had launched an

61

unstoppable initiative to behead the long-burgeoning music scene and the counterculture at large of the Mile High City.

Blatherskite first articulated his vision in the early months of 2004. Perched atop his spire of contempt, he considered his current position and pondered how it could be leveraged for access to greater power. He stood in front of a wall of floor-to-ceiling windows on the northwest-facing curve of his penthouse suite watching dusk descend over the Rocky Mountains. As the setting sun glinted off the towers of downtown Denver, he was overcome with a burning ache to control, to manipulate and to systematically destroy all that was stretched out before him. The bustling masses below, the hunkering simpletons of suburbia and the entirety of the American West spanning off into the distance — littered with the populated sores of human habitation. He wanted to uproot every inch of land on the North American continent, to boil every drop of water in the Pacific Ocean and to disintegrate every molecule of connected matter from the shores of Japan, across Asia, Russia, Europe and Africa all the way to the very core of the Earth itself. He yearned to become the President of the World, and to then corrupt every speck of dust in the vacuum of space between the planet and the sun. If he could assume the burden of immortality and disintegrate at will the entire solar system and beyond — he would gladly do so. As the MORE molecules sped through his veins and shot like quasars along the neural pathways of his brain, he was convinced that somehow, someday, this wish would come to pass.

He practically growled under the weight of his own trance "Production of MORE will be ramped up exponentially. The daily dosage for every EAR agent must be doubled. I have a world to burn."

Chapter 17

Nothing so Heavy as a Grudge

Pablo's apartment was inconspicuously tucked into the garden-level corner of what was once an all-girl boarding school. His domain was meticulously arranged with a series of shelves lining the left-hand side of the entryway, stretching all the way across the room to the foot of his bed. The books were arranged alphabetically by author and chronologically by title. William Blake, Ray Bradbury, Bill Bryson, Charles Bukowski, Joseph Campbell and on and on. On the right-hand side of the room was the doorway to the kitchen, a length of wall occupied by an antique record player, the door to the bathroom and another length of wall with a window peering foot level at what was once a playground. At the base of the window curtains, four guitars rested on stands. A vintage Gibson acoustic, a late model Takamine, a 1978 Ibanez Limited Edition electric and a Recording King Nickel-plated Resonator-style ukulele.

He sat at the edge of his bed, reminiscing about playing those old guitars — relishing in memories of wild gigs in front of naked hippies, acid casualties and speed freaks. It was during his time as a rising musician when he discovered his power.

The Mile-High Melody Festival of 1969 was quite a scene. Anti-establishment protesters demanding to be granted free entry rather than having to pony up their dope money to the man had agitated the police. At a time when public demonstrations were automatically seen by law enforcement as riot threats, triggering a bunch uneasy cops was not difficult. Floppy-haired radicals in leather sandals, bell bottoms and wicker hats were tear gassed, thumped on, arrested, detained and prosecuted. The entire Mile High Stadium Complex had been transformed from a wholesome, family-oriented, television-sanctioned hatchery of ultraviolence to a flagrant wholesale display of paranoia-sparked police brutality amid the contrasting undulations of hippie jam music and folk songs.

In the middle of Pablo's set during night three of the event, a scantily-clad flower fairy climbed onto the stage, wiggled up to him and stuck a lit joint into the side of his mouth as he sang. He inhaled and proclaimed while exhaling,

"With a tongue made of silver and a mouthful of gold
The words that ring empty are hacked up and told
And the ones who are spit on who buy and believe
Become angry and bitter at the stings of deceit"

The lyrics were by no means shocking, yet everyone in attendance decelerated into slower and slower motion until steadily creaking to a dead halt. "Man, I must really be sucking tonight" he thought while inhaling and exhaling again.

"You gotta think twice cuz things ain't what they seem,
that's why bad guys are nice and good guys are mean."

He finished the song and prayed the insanely strong weed had not permanently damaged his brain. "These fuckers all just froze on me … what the hell?"

He spat out the joint and stomped on it. The dancers, deadheads, and patchouli pixies slowly reanimated — continuing their dervish in the tear gas-tainted grass of Mile High Stadium. Slightly bewildered, they flailed as they fell back into their previous trajectories even though the music had ended. Pablo quickly launched into another tune, being careful to decline any more weed while he sang, at least until further inspection of this de-animating pot smoke-exhaling while chanting rhymes phenomenon.

Just like most songwriters of that era, Pablo wanted to gain influence within the minds of his listeners. Although mildly seductive — the accumulation of fame, riches, hordes of yes men and gaggles of money-hungry whores had little lasting appeal. He spent his time daydreaming about coming across someone about to jump off a bridge and helping them to cross it instead. He wanted to find the proverbial lost soul adrift in the darkness and ferry them to safe harbor. To teach some forgotten kid how to tie his shoes, to bait his own hook, to fix the roof over his head, to heal the holes in his heart and pass the gesture on to the next poor fucker.

Deep down he wanted to give a leg up to maybe just a few people — even one or two would do. To guide someone who had potential but no direction, imagination but no nerve, guts but no idea how to wield them. He believed that life was worth enduring as an individual if you had courage to stand up and fight when it's far easier to sit down, slump over, flop onto the ground and get pounded up the ass.

His newfound skill of freezing moments was of no help in this endeavor. Everyone he knew was already under some sort of a spell — be it LSD, marijuana or the toxic social hysteria of the era. Providence did not deliver an attentive acolyte to Pablo, but rather, a compelling ability to influence time, which then seduced his twisted sense of humor into orchestrating deranged displays of poetic justice. After years of fruitless waiting for a worthy disciple, however, he grew jaded and began augmenting his altruistic daydreams. He sometimes imagined spiteful alternatives – a shove off a bridge, a tow into a riptide, a kick in the mouth, a barb through a finger and a collapsed roof onto a bullet-ridden heart.

Chapter 18

Purple Haze

The music business has long been regarded as an artificial tree full of man-eating magpies lit up by fluorescent sunshine. It could easily be described as an overrun slaughterhouse ringing with the howls of every sort of scavenger known to the animal kingdom. For deeply mysterious reasons, the very medium that brings joy, solace and liberation to so many people also attracts those who wish to completely eradicate such notions.

These folks are the ones who run the business of music, and typically can neither play nor appreciate the art itself. One such jackal lurking among the carcasses is the archetypical music event promoter. Smarmy, shifty, beady-eyed and full of vague promises — he resents musicians for their talent and creativity, and vows to get even by ripping them off in every way possible.

In 1969, Raul Geisel was a fledgling promoter in Denver who was quickly gaining a reputation as a liar and a thief. Roughly the same age as young rising star Pablo Vasquez, their similarities ended there. By this time, Geisel had swindled Pablo and many of his contemporaries repeatedly. He was notorious for hiring local talent to open national shows and then stiffing them by claiming to have "lost his ass on this one."

After the Mile High Melody Festival, Pablo tracked Raul down in the makeshift backstage area to get paid. "Hey Geisel, how's about settling up with me? Remember that $300 we talked about?"

"Look Vasquez, I really took it in the pants this time — there's no way I can pay you when I got hundreds of people asking for refunds because the cops are out there tear gassing people."

"I heard they were rioting because the venue was oversold, and a bunch of those poor suckers simply couldn't get in."

"Oh bullshit. What the fuck do you know anyway? I'm not going to take any flak from you, Pablo. If you're such an expert, then why did people stop dancing to your music at one point today, huh? I'll tell you why — cuz it sucks. You suck. You're a goddamn nobody — now get the fuck out of my way."

Pablo stood in Geisel's path, who stopped just inches away. They stared into one another. Pablo noticed Geisel's beady eyes quivering — wanting to look away. Geisel beheld Pablo's deep set, browns that were staring through him steady and focused. With a lightning-fast twitch, Pablo's hands flew from inside his jacket pockets to an inch from Geisel's throat. "Say that again, fuckface, and I'll squeeze your chicken neck so hard those shifty little fish peepers pop right out of your skull."

"What? What the hell you fucking psycho! D … d …

don't touch me! How dare you *threaten* me … ME!" Geisel shoved past him and scurried away, disappearing among the dazed musicians, wobbling groupies, and strung-out roadies. The same flower fairy who shoved the joint in his mouth during his set strolled up. "Aw shit, man that was awesome! Don't sweat that asshole, here — have a toke. By the way — you were great today." She handed him yet another joint as Geisel's voice ricocheted at him from down the hallway. "Fuck you, Vasquez — you sonofabitch! You'll never work in this town again! I ain't no fucking thief! And I … I … I uh … don't do business with *thugs* like you!" As the echoes ricocheted about him like outhouse flies, he pondered the cherry at the end of the joint that was burning slowly, steadily and seemingly with purpose.

Later that night, Pablo had devised a plan and decided to test it out immediately. The afterhours party that night took place in the green room which was nothing more than the locker room for the visiting team that was in town to play the Denver Broncos. A room normally reserved for world-class athletes was instead overrun with acid heads, pill freaks, music floozies and all manner of counter cultural reprobates. Most were using the doorless lockers as make out booths or quasi hot boxes for corralling pot smoke. Pablo approached a cluster of heads at the far end of the locker room, encircled around none other than the night's headlining star — one Mr. Jimi Hendrix. "Hey, can someone spare a hit of a joint for a jonesing fool over here?" The small group parted, turning to regard the guy who played a supporting set, got a bunch of fans to play "freeze frame," threatened to choke the promoter and was somehow still in the building.

"Sure brother," exhaled Hendrix, "take the horns off this one. Great set earlier, by the way. Dig it, man."

Pablo accepted the joint and said, "thank you my man,"

as he inhaled. When he exhaled, he continued, "it was a stone-cold pleasure opening up for you, Jimi." At this point he expected some sort of momentary human de-animation he'd witnessed earlier, but instead everyone kept chattering on, fawning over Jimi until the guy to Pablo's right said, "hey man don't bogart that dope, pass it along bro."

The next time it was his turn to hit the joint, he remembered the exact circumstances and instead of talking as he exhaled, he spoke a rhyming verse of one of his songs:

"Your mama was a wolf your daddy was an ape,
A baron of filth in a garbage bag cape,
You showed up with your feral girlfriend on your wing,
And that is why we don't have nice things."

He was halfway through the verse and people began to smile and snicker at the imagery. He took another toke, inhaled and then exhaled again. "

Your vision is blurred your hearing is shot,
Your language is slurred like a pirate on pot,
You blow snot when you laugh and you spit when you speak,
And that is why we don't have nice things."

Everyone in earshot — the three hippies to his left, the dude to his right, the two gals next to him who were starstruck and Jimi himself had all froze mid expression. Jimi had just begun laughing and Pablo took advantage of the moment to peer into the soul of a living legend. The corners of Jimi's eyes curled upwards as did his grin. All seven people were still frozen, except Jimi who slowly reached forward with his left hand and placed it on the side of Pablo's right elbow. He whispered lowly, "You got some kind of power, brother. Far fucking out, man."

Chapter 19

Cold Revenge

The next day, Denver was rife with rumors about how the promoter of the Mile-High Melody Festival oversold the event. The murmurings were grave, with undertones of disgust at how some selfish suit caused a bunch of freshly-swindled music fans to be harassed, molested and jailed by an overzealous police response.

In a hasty attempt to save his reputation, Raul Geisel held a press conference at the Brown Palace Hotel in the heart of downtown Denver the night after the festival. The Churchill Bar was bustling with reporters, camera operators, technical lackeys and even a few local heads who were lucky enough to catch wind of the impromptu event. Geisel sat at long table with the head of his security team to his left and the Denver Chief of Police to his right. His efforts to appear cavalier and nonchalant were causing him to sweat and fidget.

Denver Post reporter Bill Hosokawa began the barrage of questions. "Mr. Geisel, how do you answer these rumors about overselling the Denver Pop Festival for personal gain?"

He shifted in his seat, ever so slightly "Obviously these rumors are nothing more than hysteria perpetuated by a few troublemakers who were trying to ruin a good thing for a whole lot of people."

The Chief of Police stood by in silence, a large wad of 100 dollar bills crinkling in his front pocket inspired his compliance.

Meanwhile, Pablo Vasquez entered the lobby with a freshly-twisted joint in his mouth. The night before, he'd become intimate with the weed fairy who was now an accomplice. He held a walkie talkie to his face and pressed the "talk" button, "OK Luna, get ready. When I say the word, pull the switch."

She chirped into her walkie talkie, "Sure thing, daddy-o!" The radio fuzz bounced off the concrete walls as she crouched in the dim light of the hotel basement next to the power panel for the entire building.

It was Geisel's head of security's turn at the microphone. Assurances of promotion to profit-sharing partner in the company had him dizzy with conviction. "I personally counted the final door revenues and crossed referenced them with how many tickets were sold. Mr. Geisel's numbers are on to the dollar."

Pablo lit the joint, inhaled deeply and walked into the Churchill Bar. He eased the door shut behind him and exhaled.

"Liars and thieves retire into grief
And buyers of belief are just queefs in the briefs."

The pot smoke rolled across the room like a wave of laudanum. The head of security began to slur his words as the pitch of his voice deepened and the cadence of his talking slowed. The entire room began to decelerate as Pablo took another hit. He held it in, ordered a simple command of "Five" into his walkie talkie and exhaled again.

> *"Five you're all alive*
> *Four look at the floor*
> *Three it's time to sleep*
> *Two right on cue*
> *One you're all done."*

At that moment, Luna pulled downward on the main power lever. The Churchill Bar went dark and every witness and camera was rendered temporarily blind. Pablo made his way towards Geisel's table via the light of his Zippo. He stood before a stupefied, frozen face he would love to simply smash into a pulp, but instead he reached into his rucksack and produced a cardboard sign — yellow poster board with block letters in black stencil. He propped it up against Geisel's nose, leaving just his eyes peering over the top edge, and then Pablo backed out of the Churchill bar with haste.

Luna cranked the power back on moments later at Pablo's command — just as everyone in the Churchill Bar was reanimating and regaining consciousness. They were stunned, shocked and stupefied to see that the man who was just defending his innocence with utter certainty had suddenly, somehow, out of thin air produced a sign that he was now cowering behind — barely peeking over the top. The murmur quickly grew into an uproar as newspaper columnists, radio journalists, camera operators from the three major network news channels and a very confused bartender assimilated the words on the sign.

"I AM LYING. THESE MEN WILL MURDER ME. PLEASE HELP."

Chapter 20

Dessert

The ensuing melee was borderline chaos as the three men at the table were initially clueless about the sign's message. Some in the room slowly backed away, others ran for the door while the bartender began motioning frantically to the police officers who were already on site at the behest of their Chief.

Geisel was baffled, publicly humiliated and privately terrified. He tried playing the whole thing off as a practical joke of his own design because, you know, the absurdity of the accusation of "overselling the show." The Chief of Denver Police was furious and laughed in his face when he asked for his bribe money back. His head of security quit and took the rest of the staff with him to start a new company. Undaunted, he resolved to carry on as a promoter as he had worked hard to make serious inroads with some of the biggest names in rock and roll.

Pablo vowed to stalk Geisel and to keep sabotaging the greaseball until his reputation as a concert promoter was irreversibly destroyed. This resulted in a series of froze-and-stoned-poetry -stunts that systematically achieved just that.

In June of 1970, the power suddenly went out along concourse C of Denver Stapleton Airport. Raul Geisel was there to greet a band called The Who — a quartet of rising stars that was scheduled to play Mammoth Gardens the following evening. Hearsay of their arrival on Continental Airlines was afoot, so numerous press representatives, a gaggle of hysterical fans and few aspiring groupies were there just in case the rumors were correct. As Pete Townsend, John Entwistle, Roger Daltrey and Keith Moon began to enter the concourse from the jetway, Pablo began enunciating lines of poetry from his hidden post behind one of the support columns. The concourse was built on a granite floor and had tiles running up every wall to the ceiling. His voice echoed across the massive hallway with a sinister lilt:

"Crime has many faces some ugly and some grim
I wouldn't bet my aces on me if I were him."

Then, a thick gust of marijuana smoke overtook the scene as everyone in earshot began to de-animate and the voice continued:

"Stealing is like killing with cruel drawn-out pain
No longer am I willing to ever be fooled again."

There was a short burst of walkie talkie fuzz, a muttered grunt and then the lights went out and were replaced by the dim glow of the emergency power-outage fixtures.

Pablo darted deftly between statuesque bystanders to the check-in counter and fetched two previously stashed sheets of thin wood connected by two straps at one end. As he was affixing the assembly to Geisel, he noticed that the entire band had entered the area and become paralyzed by his spell save for Keith Moon, who kept walking into Roger Daltrey, backing up and repeating the action. He was clearly hammered beyond belief. On the third collision with Roger, he stopped and rested his head on his singer's shoulder, content to watch a man in a trench coat and a wide-brimmed cowboy hat hang a sandwich board sign upon a famous promoter amid a room full of people frozen between breaths. "Aye mate" he queried "what's this all about?"

"Go ahead and tell them" Pablo muttered "they'll never believe your drunk ass anyways."

A few seconds later when power was restored, Geisel was standing with hand outstretched to greet the rock and roll quartet from England, yet somehow, he was wearing a body-length sign. Scrawled across the front, a strange message:

"THE WHO ARE GUILTY.
THEY PAID MANSON
TO DO IT."

On the back, another note:

"BECAUSE
THEY
HATE
TATE."

Pete Townsend reeled back and punched Geisel in the jaw, knocking him out cold. Later that night, as Keith moon tried to relate what he witnessed between mouthfuls of decorative flowers from the hotel lobby, his bandmates simply shook their heads and gave him another beer.

Vasquez drove the final nail into the coffin of Geisel's promoting career in 1971. The day after mayhem broke out during a Jethro Tull concert at Red Rocks amphitheater, Geisel was once again fielding questions as to how and why such a debacle came to be. It was his show after all, and somehow 1,000 or so fans couldn't get in as the event was oversold. There were hundreds of fake tickets that were clearly third and fourth generation photocopies printed onto cheap construction paper. After hordes of hypervigilant hippies holding these bunk forgeries were turned away, they formed into compact clusters and stormed the fences — determined to experience the acoustic magic of Red Rocks.

Once again, the trigger happy Denver Police Department deployed tear gas canisters into a chaotic scene. Were it not for the effort of the band to calm them down, the sacred site would have been sullied by a full-blown riot. Instead, the band persevered through their set — led by singer Ian Anderson and his flute playing — that he somehow, miraculously, made work with rock and roll.

Geisel was arrested after the concert on suspicion of fraud, released the next day and arraigned later that week in Denver County Court. The Judge was decidedly anti-rock music and leered down at Geisel with consternation. Her voice boomed at him, "Mr. Raul Geisel, you have been accused of Defrauding the Public, Reckless Endangerment and Inciting a Riot. How do you answer these charges?"

"Your honor," he whimpered, "I was framed ... someone, I don't know who, is out to get me. They are trying to ruin my reputation by printing bogus tickets and scalping them to music fans."

"Mr. Geisel, as I see it, your reputation is already ruined after these ridiculous public stunts you keep pulling."

"Your honor, those are perpetrated by the people who are out to get me. They keep sabotaging me with some kind of ... of ... public hypnosis."

"Sir, I will not be mocked in my own courtroom with such a ridiculous claim. I do not appreciate being blatantly lied to." She was starting to clench her jowls with fury as Geisel began to tremble. Meanwhile, Pablo sat in the back row of the courtroom, bowing his hatless head to discreetly light a joint from within his trench coat.

"Your honor ... I ... I ..."

Pablo stood up, put his hat back on to obscure his face, took a deep toke and then stunned the courtroom with a waft of pot smoke blown beneath tightly rhymed couplets:

*"He's a counterfeit leech a sly thief in the night
He won't do or teach, and he damn well can't fight."*

When she heard the disturbance, the judge lifted her gavel, but before she bring it down onto the sound block her arm began to slow down mid-arc. Pablo blew out another gust of ganja smoke and continued his screed:

*"Not even honest when he's muted this art parasite
A filibustering galoot a goddamn blatherskite."*

There were no cameras present in courtrooms back then, so Pablo had the luxury of affixing Geisel's new signage with illuminated clarity. This one was a Mickey Mouse hat with a piece of poster board affixed to the top - taped between both ears for support. It bore a customized message on the front.

"HEY BITCH.
YOUR PLACE IS
IN THE HOME."

On the back, an equally succinct note for a full courtroom.

"FUCK

YOU
ALL"

Raul Geisel was found guilty, sentenced to a short time in jail and then ordered to perform a lengthy degree of community service. This led to roadside cleanup which he parlayed into his job as a meter maid. His entry-level baptism into the dysfunctional clusterfuck known as municipal government was like hawking a bacteria-ridden flugie into a filthy toilet bowl of warm piss. A rapid acclimation gave way to a deliberate climb to the top of the administrative pecking order of Denver all the way to the head of an agency of his own creation — a position he held uncontested 30-some-odd years later.

Chapter 21

Kindred Spirits

Cricket and Earl cruised along in silence. Once she realized the car was about to run out of gas, she suggested some tactical analysis.

They pulled into an abandoned warehouse complex in Commerce City just northeast of downtown Denver. The stale stench of mass processed low-rate dog food wafted through their open windows from the nearby Urina plant. Earl was a tad drunk from the evening's battle with The Gasser, and the smell made him gag. "Whuuulp." He broke the silence between them with the charm of a dry heave.

"Hah!" Cricket cackled. "Are you gonna fuckin' puke now or what?"

"N … no .... I just…"

"This ain't my goddamn car. Go for it."

"I just want to thank you for saving my ass back there."

"You looked like you needed a drink."

"I guess you might say that I've got a bit of a problem."

"Motherfuckin' shit man," curse words rolled out of her mouth like wet marbles. "You and me both." Cricket regarded Earl for a moment, noting the square jawline, blonde-ish beard stubble, triangular nose and humble eyes. "You know," she continued, "for a guy who knocks 'em back like you do, you don't look half bad."

"I've always been a beer drinker but lately my consumption has escalated to say the least. Ever since this sonic belch blasting thing started, I've been on a fairly serious bender."

"I've been hoping I wouldn't have to bring it up, but now that you mention it, can you please explain to me what the fuck your deal is?"

Earl strained through his periphery to secretly appreciate her profile. He had watched dozens of times as she burst through the doors of The Joker and prowled about, seemingly protected from the drooling savages by an invisible force field. He would trace her movements from behind his bangs, pretending to be fixated on the beer bottle in front of him. His pulse would quicken as she swilled tequila and ululated like a coyote as the neon light glinted off the sheen of her raincoat.

"Something happened to me recently. I was hammered one night after drinking a shitload of beer. A fight broke out at the bar. Some half-assed gangsters were thumping on this hipster guy. I tried to help and instead of yelling, a belch blast came out that flattened the place. Freaked the hell out of me. Probably worse than the rest."

"So, it wasn't a bunch of M-80s that busted up The Joker after all?"

"'Fraid not."

"And now you're trying to stop The Gasser, huh? All by your lonesome? That putrid sonofabitch is one sick motherfucker. Attacking pregnant women, trying to kill them and their unborn children? Fuck that. You can count me in. I'll back you up 100%." She took a tube of red lipstick out of her overcoat pocket and deftly applied a swipe to the bottom brim of her mouth. She smeared her lips together, then smacked them apart with a clap that sounded like a suction cup being yanked away from a panel of wet glass. Her tough bitch exterior was beginning to soften. "Man, I could really go for a beer right now."

"Yeah me too. I hate running out. Like the saying goes, I always try to 'save one for later.'"

Cricket's head and torso whipped to the right to face Earl straight on. "Huh? What? Where did you hear that?"

"Hear what?"

"That saying. 'Save one for later.'"

"Well, I sort of picked it up recently. See, I have this friend. He's been helping me figure this shit out. You know, teaching me how to focus and how to … well … how to not be such a meek little pussy." Earl said it with equal parts self-loathing and newly discovered nerve.

Cricket laughed again, throwing her head back and slapping her thighs. "Lemme guess … long brown duster, wide-brimmed cowboy hat, thick beard and a poetic weed smoking habit, right?"

"Uh, yeah — how'd you … "

"I know him. You and I have more in common than you may think. Pablo has a penchant for finding strays and turning them into vicious beasts."

Chapter 22

Kiss Me You Fool

They abandoned the blue Challenger among the dilapidated industrial husks of north Denver and headed back downtown on foot. Cricket ambled nimbly alongside Earl who, for a drunk guy, was getting along well save for the occasional stumble. "We should take side streets. Stay in the shadows. They'll be looking for you."

"I ... ah ...ulp ... I agree ... BLUUURP." Residual belches were a problem, as they tended to sneak up on Earl long after the fact. Every car alarm to the end of the next intersection began wailing and they took off in a sprint. Halfway down the block, mid stride, they both started to laugh.

"Hey asshole," Cricket chortled, "can you try and keep a lid on it — at least until we're indoors!?"

By now Earl had begun developing the skill of belch-talking — the act of forming words and sentences with guttural expulsion rather than exhalation. He belted out a loud blast that thundered like a plastic bucket of large rocks being dumped into a steel wheelbarrow. "YEAH SORRY

NO PROBLEM!" The sound wave radiated across the neighborhood and erupted into a car alarm cacophony.

"Aw, you fucking asshole" she barked teasingly, then took his hand and darted down an alleyway —yanking Earl after her and leading them towards Capitol Hill. "Where the fuck do you live, Mr. Manners?"

"It's Danners."

"Huh?"

"Earl Danners."

As he ran next to Cricket, her hand clasped tight around his, tassels of drool trailed from the corners of his mouth and flapped next to his ears like spaghetti. He felt weightless, like he was running on thin air.

As they stepped into the elevator in Earl's building, Cricket thought maybe she detected a tiny hint of a familiar stench. But as they ascended, it vanished.

Earl was exhausted and still a bit drunk, yet his flophouse-like digs still managed to make him self-conscious. "I wasn't expecting company. The only other person who's ever been here is Pablo."

"Yeah I can tell." Cricket counted over half a dozen empty Quasimodo Gold boxes. I see he introduced you to QM."

"To what?"

"Quasimodo Gold. Wisconsin Sewage. Whatever you want to call it. The shit grows on you, don't it?"

"Yep, and I saved one for later — more than one, actually. Want to drink a beer with me?"

"Yeah sure. Why the fuck not?"

They sat side by side on Earl's couch and Cricket sipped while Earl chugged. His long-constrained social functionality was now becoming unbridled and seemed to know no bounds. "So ... how'd you meet Pablo?"

"He's kind of like my second father."

And just like that, he abandoned his nerve and backpedaled into the safety of silence.

The shock and raw trepidation must have shown on his face. Cricket gave him another ribbing. "Aw c'mon you fuckin' sissy. That don't mean shit. The old man is practically a ghost. I think all that weed has warped his brain. He sneaks around and I only run into him at night. He's always looking over his shoulder like he's about to get jumped and yammering on about how the EAR top brass has got it in for him."

"Actually, there may be some truth to that. He's talked to me several times about stuff like 'people being out there who want to shut us up for good' and shit like that."

"Yeah? Well whatever ... I mean, I miss the old bastard. He says I gotta keep a distance cuz I'm putting myself in danger by hanging out with him. I just think he's sick of having me follow him around like a lost mutt and having to do damage control every time I go on a tequila rampage and start blinding motherfuckers and taking their shit."

"At least you're a drinker too. Around you I don't feel so bad for pounding them back, ya know?" They tapped their QM cans together and sipped in silence.

"Yeah that fucking Pablo. One helluva songwriter that guy." She pulled out her flask of tequila and absent-mindedly took a swig. "I met him years ago when I used to go to concerts a lot. "I guess it was pretty apparent that I was a fuckup with no friends. Once I turned into a regular at his shows, he took a liking to me and then eventually we became friends. I owe a lot to that ornery sonofabitch."

"Yeah? How so?" Earl extended his right hand across their laps, motioning to the flask in Cricket's left hand.

"You don't want any of this until I wipe my spit off the nozzle. Trust me."

"Why not?"

"Just gimme a second, goddammit. I'm getting to that." She took another pull and clunked the flask down onto the coffee table next to the beer cans. She breathed in deep and exhaled with a huff. "I have poisonous saliva. Deadly drool. Toxic slobber. Spiteful Spit." Earl said nothing, instead he kept sucking back beer and listening, fascinated.

"If my saliva comes in contact with skin, it stings really bad, and if I spit in your eye, you'd go blind for a minute or two. One night, while hanging out with Pablo and drinking tequila, he made me laugh and I accidentally gleaked. It flew straight into his eye. He started screaming, holding his head and thrashing around in pain. I thought he was fucking with me, but he was serious. Up until then he didn't even know about my little problem."

Earl was captivated. "Holy shit, so you've got a BANE too?"

"Yeah, and that's why I can't kiss you right now even though I'd really like to. I don't want to hurt you."

There is was again, that strange feeling of bravado that was systematically eclipsing his cowardice. Earl decided to take another chance, while he still had one. "I'm pretty toxic myself. Most of the time I'm either hungover or on the way to catching a functional buzz again. Remember what they taught in math and science class? That sometimes two negatives can equal a positive?"

"No. I hated school."

Earl leaned in and kissed Cricket softly on her crimson lips. He braced for a surge of searching pain as she pressed into him and slowly opened her mouth. There was no sting of poison or excruciating attack of agony — only the melding of warm, wet flesh — a succulent billowing of lips and tongues awash in the flavors of rotgut tequila and skunk beer. After a few moments they pulled apart. Earl couldn't help it as a tiny little smile forced its way into the framework of his face. It was his first kiss, and her first kiss that didn't result in some terrible mandibular disaster. Cricket didn't fight the grin taking over her face as a tear swelled from her left duct and trailed down her cheek.

"Watch out," she smiled, "those are toxic too."

Chapter 23

Hell Hath no Fury

Just as Pablo and Luna's romance began amid madness, so it continued in discord and met its demise with a blowout. It was a repeating cycle of reconciliation, whirlwind lust, attempted domesticity, tumultuous bickering and bitter separation.

Although in her younger years Luna was a wild-eyed and willing accomplice, her desire for modern luxuries and lavish excursions had long since eclipsed the novelty of "living an alternative lifestyle." Her repeated attempts to get Pablo to use his power to illegally acquire money and possessions were met with resistance which soured into resentment.

"Goddammit Pablo, I can't go on living like a ragamuffin vagabond. We're not kids anymore. I want a nice house, a vacation, limousine rides, a fur coat and a chihuahua that rides in a little gold-stitched purse."

"Aw c'mon now — that's all a bunch of bullshit and you know it."

"Oh, fuck off you selfish bastard. You could pull one of your dope-smoking paralysis stunts and make us a million bucks in a day, but instead you're just slinging that sorry ass Arizona ditch weed and I'm over here eating cans of generic soup. Anyone else in your shoes would steal a bunch of money and go live high on the hog, for Christ's sake."

"I've told you a hundred times, I'm not doing that because stealing ain't right. You think it's OK to just milk the cow through the fence whenever it suits you, but I'm telling you it's wrong goddammit."

"There you go again with your podunk shitkicker anecdotes. I'll tell you what you fuckin' coward, you goddamn bum — I'm gonna go live in style and leave your broke ass here in the dust — playing your pathetic little songs in these shitty-ass Denver dive bars. I'm gonna go out and find myself a *real* man. I'm gonna be licking his balls while you're sitting here playing with yourself. Haha!"

"Oh yeah? You couldn't lick your lips."

On the way towards the door she grabbed his Takamine acoustic guitar, stopped at the threshold and glared at him, her face turning bright red.

"Don't you fucking dare, you crazy bitch!" He couldn't tell if she was going to smash it or take it with her as she ran out into the night. Instead, she flung it at his head with alarming velocity. He ducked and it hit the wall behind him and then clamored to the floor as the door slammed behind her. It was broken just below the headstock and dented on the front side of the body. His beloved six string lay there mangled, like a swan with a broken neck, while the maw of a sinkhole began roaring open inside him. It was an overwhelming situation, and he fell to his knees under the thick ooze of a sadness so heavy he literally couldn't stand it. He felt like he had been dipped in tar and run over by a herd of horses.

Meanwhile, Luna was raving mad and tad gleeful that she'd finally acted out her frustrations. She decided that a visit to an old friend would be just the thing to seal her vindication and show stupid-ass Pablo Vasquez who's really in charge.

The next day she stood at the front desk in the ground floor lobby of EAR. "I'm here to see Raul Geisel," she chirped.

The attending agent's brain had been systematically bleached clean with copious amounts of blather and MORE — and he replied with a robotic, glassy-eyed tone, "Do you have an appointment?"

"No, asshead," Luna was smug, "just tell Mr. Geisel I have some very important information about a person who was covertly harassing him some time ago."

The interior of the EAR Headquarters building was a conical column that rose twelve stories into the Denver skyline like a giant whitewashed pylon. The curved walkways and railings of each level were visible from the lobby foyer and accessed via stairwell or diagonal elevator. The ground level spanned a circumference a dozen times the diameter of the penthouse — the floor of which was a thick, continuous lens of two-way mirrored glass. Looking up, Luna could see only the reflection of 11 sets of railings and herself as a tiny speck in the middle of the lobby — craning her neck to peer upward. Meanwhile, Blatherskite stood above her, and could read the trepidation on her face from 120 feet up through the telescopic feature imbedded beneath his feet.

Minutes later, she was sitting across from Geisel on the top floor of the EAR Headquarters building. His bloodshot eyes, thinning hair and pale skin gave her pause — he was almost unrecognizable — but it was too late to turn back, so she committed to orchestrating the bribe. "You are Raul Geisel, correct?"

"Well, it depends who's asking … heh heh heh," his chuckle was like a rusty coil on an old screen door. "I go by that name … among others." He noted her slightly graying hair, her glowing feminine facial features and svelte yet curvy figure. He was debating on whether to rape her, kill her or both.

Luna proceeded to recount the events of 30 years prior — the public humiliations that knocked Geisel off his pedestal and into a life of menial jobs, mid-level pencil pushing positions and now to his power-obsessed status as the head of a nefarious wing of civic government. The very utterance of those scenarios made Geisel furious, madder than Luna was the prior evening by many degrees. "So … Miss Luna, if that really is your name, what can you tell me about the perpetrator of these heinous crimes that ruined my career and nearly drove me to suicide?"

"Well, sir, I am more than willing to share that information with you, and I am offering to do so with just one tiny stipulation."

"And what, pray tell, would that be?"

"I am asking for a small stipend — a courier fee if you will — of one million dollars. Not a penny more."

"Not a penny more?"

"Not one red cent more." She smiled and clasped her hands together like an innocent widow asking for a bank loan to pay for her dead hubby's gravestone.

Geisel's tone darkened from measured and cordial to slightly menacing. "I like that word."

Luna's acute sense of denial kicked in. There was nothing wrong here. Nothing at all. "What word?"

"MORE." He leered at her while leaning over his desk. He reached into the top drawer with his right hand and pulled out a tray decorated with four pre-cut lines of MORE. "Who the fuck do you think you are, you stupid bitch." He was trembling with rage. "You think you can come into my fortress, drudge up the most humiliating times of my life and then try to bribe me out of a million bucks with some bullshit information?"

"Oh but Mr. Geisel, you see, I believe you will be quite pleased with what you learn. And after all, won't it be nice to finally have closure?"

As she spoke, he pulled a two-pronged device from his pocket — a set of short black metallic straws held by sleeves that were spaced about as far apart as the width of a nasal septum. Geisel used it to deftly inhale two lines of MORE at one time with a fierce, eye-popping snort. He massaged his nostrils together while sniffling, then leaned in close to Luna's face — leering into her eyes as he sputtered, "Closure? There is no fucking closure. Ever, ever, ever!"

He then took a deep breath, leering and wincing as he prepared to warp her will into acquiescence with a mind-bending harangue of nonsense. "I remember your face you filthy, cock gargling little whore. You skittered from one sorry-assed guitar slinging loser to another back in the day. You never were to smart, were you? Now … I am going to ruin what's left of your tiny little mind."

"You thread on my bare and tread on my care and head cut my hair with dead nuts and wares. I seethe as you breathe and heave at your knees and wheeze like a breeze of swarm flies and fleas. Don't wink at my think or pink up my stink or

I'll chink to the brink 'til your soul's in the clink."

Luna's grip on her mental resolve was systematically being forced loose like threads on the lid of a rusted-shut mason jar. Blatherskite began his screed again, this time twice as fast with his face contorting as though he was being electrocuted during the centrifugal crush of a g-force simulator. By the sixth run through his litany of bilge, he could tell that her will had been cracked, and she had begun the inevitable slide into his trance. He then shifted gears from somewhat understandable chatter to complete gibberish — an overdrive mode that was meant to drive the listener insane — temporarily or otherwise.

"Scrapillaponding dishooey sassensfractured nonfrunct, switchglipping yelltides congort wong gavel hypes. Lubbertubing hippertures pin garverstrations and kibs, jivastate bilgrapings, yabbigasterish gribs, beeshing mammertides and vackful whorezacked pongfillatures."

Blatherskite repeated the meaningless mantra as the cadence, camber and tone eclipsed Luna's will to think clearly and then splintered her ego into a scattered, hopeless puzzle. "Now, my sweet little dried up pile of pixie dust … tell me just who this elusive person was who ruined my chance at rock and roll greatness. Spit it out, damn you!"

Luna sputtered, struggling to articulate — her green eyes swimming in their sockets like she'd just been brained with a cast iron pan. "P … Puh … Pah … Pab …" she couldn't get the name out at first, and then … "Pablo."

"I knew it, I fucking knew it. God damn that motherfucking asshole. I'm gonna find him and string him up by his heels and beat him to death with what's left of your rotting corpse you filthy conniving little …" as he was carrying on, Luna continued speaking, explaining in detail her role as accomplice in each mission. Blatherskite continued to rant, but then he noticed she was still talking so he abruptly shut up and took it all in. Luna was speaking candidly with complete abandon and disregard for her circumstances, like a child talking in her sleep.

"That's how we humiliated you, made everyone hate you and we both thought it was quite funny ..." He took his double-barreled snorting straw, reared back and then thrust it forward, straight through her left eye socket and into the frontal cortex of her brain. Luna continued talking as though nothing happened. "We kept it secret for years, laughing about how you went from socialite hot shot to groveling meter maid." She continued to yammer while blood spurted from her eye socket all over his face. He then yanked a switchblade from his pocket, flicked it open and swung forward in a wailing arc — slicing her throat open from ear to ear. Her head bent back, and her esophagus opened with more spurts of blood flying out accompanied by little puffs of air that were headed for her mouth but never made it.

Her diatribe ended at last, as the blood that was flowing to and from her brain was instead all over the floor, the desk and the face of her killer. EAR agents were summoned as Blatherskite basked in the intoxicating thrill of what he had, alas, uncovered about his regretful past.

"Vasquez," He growled through clenched teeth, "first I'm going to ruin you, and then I am going to kill you."

Chapter 24

Occupational Incentives

Blatherskite stood over Luna's body as it drained of blood — the hatred searing through his veins alongside the compounds of copious amounts of MORE. As his fists trembled and his face glowed with rage like the cherry of a burning cigarette, his brain began to light up with ideas.

He returned to the dope tray on his desk and rather than snorting the two remaining lines of MORE, he sucked up just one. The thrill of murder had awakened his libido, and he didn't want to risk killing that too. "Always save one for later," he chuckled.

Raul Geisel's naked hips slapping against the lifeless skin of Luna's limp pelvis sounded like a warped wooden oar being repeatedly smacked upon a pile of mud. His hands continually slipped outward as he attempted to balance himself by placing his palms into the expanding pool of her blood. Just as he was climaxing, he righted himself at an angle above her torso and lurched forward with a final thrust. His hands slid out from beneath his shoulders once again — causing him to faceplant into Luna and bonk his forehead on her dead skull. A team of on-duty EAR agents scurried into the room just as Blatherskite was screaming his frustrations and psychoses into her blank face, "God damn you stupid fucking whore ... I hate you!" he hollered as his toxic DNA shot into her desecrated womb.

The security detail were veterans of the EAR staff and seasoned MORE junkies who were easily convinced over a tray of white lines that the mess at hand was the result of an attack upon their leader. "You see what happens when you let one of the polluters in here without a cavity search and a thorough interrogation? The fucking cunt tried to stab me in the heart." The EAR agents each sniffled, rubbed their noses and slipped into a focused haze. "Clean up this fucking mess and then take the body down to the basement kitchen and put it in the walk-in cooler. Stand by for further instructions." Wrapped in the northwest-facing wall of windows curtains and crumpled between the boots of two EAR agents, Luna's body descended back down the circular, cavernous structure and into the bowels of the building.

Blatherskite logged into the company mainframe and did some research into the human resource data files. He pinpointed the one recruit in each of the 10 squadrons with the lowest aptitude for empathy and the highest display of sociopathic traits. Each man was summoned from the barracks, and the group was assembled in a line along the far side of the white-tiled basement mess hall. Adjacent to the kitchen, the area had been cleared of furniture, and was simply an open space of glossy white ceramic lit up by sterile overhead LED fixtures.

Blatherskite stood in front of a row of stainless steel appliances — an oven, circular burners, a flattop, storage cabinets and refrigeration units — all installed at uniform height and depth. In the center of the kitchen stood a stainless steel prep table with Blatherskite on the far side facing his men — each one slated for a face to face chit chat with their jabbering leader.

The first EAR recruit, freshly fazed after the latest orientation assembly, was called forth to the table. He approached the cold silver steel to face Blatherskite and two racing stripe-sized lines of MORE laid out on the silvery surface between them. "You have been summoned here because you exhibit the potential to carry out the will of EAR with superior resolve." The agent blinked with a flat gawp that was pasty under the fluorescent bulbs. "I am inducting you and 11 of your compatriots into a top-secret, classified squadron. As we begin the ritual, you shall inhale two bonus rails of our sacred MORE. Once I begin the invocation of a new modality upon you — you must chant with me."

Blatherskite handed over his double-barreled nostril throttler. The promising young agent, rigid with the intensity of encroaching psychosis, took the implement and leaned forward. As he began to snort, Blatherskite launched into a ceremonial rant.

"I am a servant of the Environmental Agency of Restrictions. I will vanquish the polluters of this jurisdiction. I will envelop their crimes which deafen and blind. Their blood shall be my quenching brine, their flesh devoured to become mine." After the second incantation, the agent stood up — wide eyed and straight and Blatherskite broke the cadence. "Chant with me now, my son!" He bellowed. The agent began chanting along, quickly slipping into a deep, impenetrable trance.

The remaining nine agents and the two members of the security detail were given identical benedictions, systematically locked into trances and directed back to their places along the edge of the mess where the white floor tile met the wall. Echoes of their chanting ricocheted about the room in a cacophony of rising chaos as they yapped in unison. Blatherskite emerged from the walk-in cooler at the far end of the kitchen pushing a utility cart — upon which rode Luna's body swaddled by the blood-soaked drapes. He guided the cart to the center of the mess hall, locked the wheels and continued chanting along with his troops. " ... *Their blood shall be my quenching brine, their flesh devoured to become mine* ... "

Circling the cart counterclockwise, he began peeling back the drenched layers of fabric with his left hand while pulling a silver whistle from his pocket with his right. As the last layer fell away, he stopped at the 12 o'clock position. Luna's limp corpse was now revealed — splayed out between him and his newly galvanized squadron. He began chanting louder and louder, nearly to a scream, and as the voices of his men escalated with his, he raised the whistle to his cracked lips and blew it with a mighty *"thweeeeeet."*

The men instantly halted their mantra, frozen between impulse and idiocy. "And now — my slavering brethren — I present to you the remains of one of Denver's most reviled. The Princess of the Polluters herself who, not two hours ago, attempted to murder me — your eminent leader. Now, upon my command, I shall order you rip her limb from limb! We will devour her supple flesh to fuel our quest to rid this city of her kind. Her sinews will make you saintly, her blood will make you brave and her guts will make you fearless!" Blatherskite's final screamed syllable rippled back and forth and finally dissipated until the mess hall was nearly silent save for the heavy breathing of 13 sociopathic men. He slowly brought the whistle back up to his mouth, inhaled deeply and blew into it — releasing a shriek of commanding trills flying forth at 100 decibels.

The agents of EAR descended onto Luna like a pack of hyenas. The squishing sound of flesh being shoved into moaning mouths mixed with the snapping of bones and the ripping of skin sounded like her body had been dropped into a giant blender set on the low speed.

Raul Geisel looked on approvingly, glimmering with pride as blood, guts and bits of body were slopped about and gobbled up before him. After a few minutes, a spirited tussle between the two security detail agents ensued. They were having a tug of war over her heart, which, slick with blood, slipped away from them, flew through the air and landed between Blatherskite's feet with a splat.

He picked up her heart, admired it for a moment, and then sunk his teeth in — ripping away a red, sinewy bite.

Chapter 25

Invitation to the Blues

The black hole of yearning and remorse that began imploding inside Pablo's guts told him all he needed to know. Luna was gone, and she wasn't coming back. His usual regimen of weed and cerebral propaganda a la OG Kush and William Blake would not see him through this one. He needed more than herbal distractions and spiritual aberrations. He was compelled to immerse himself in mourning and loss by hearing the echoes of his own heartache belted, wailed and cast forth by a master of an elusive craft.

El Chapo was the final lower downtown holdout of old Denver. The district was nicknamed "LoDo" to have snappy appeal to future soccer Moms and big business-bound frat boys. The club was the lone stalwart of genuine music in an otherwise soulless grid of marketing hype, major league sports broadcasts and overpriced junk food. Somehow amid gentrification and generic redevelopment, El Chapo managed to maintain its claim to a corner of the busiest intersection in five square miles.

This room featured the very best in old-school blues and

jazz players. Stevie Ray Vaughan knockoffs with copycat belt buckle hats and thick-strung Stratocasters were told quite plainly to go fuck themselves. When Pablo darkened the El Chapo doorway for the first time in months, the regulars who were hunkered over the bar seemed to sense his anguish — and he was spared the pain of formality. He found his old spot at the end of the wood, just after the elbow. It was the perfect perch for surveying the thin room which hosted a run of 17 stools that were bolted to the floor. At the south end of the room sat a tidy, compact stage. The room was a wreck of a rectangle stretched out like a giant tattered box for a pair of very long, worn out shoes. The mirror behind the bar was permanently stained from a century of cigarette smoke and on any given shift, whomever was bartending was easily the ugliest person present.

Red-eye Robinson was strumming his way through a set of original tunes — a one-man band churning out a hybrid of Mississippi Delta Blues and tremolo-heavy New Orleans swamp rock. He kept time with both feet on makeshift contraptions while wailing away on his Dobro slide guitar and singing with forlorn conviction — simultaneously possessed by anguish, sadness and measured rage. He stomped the downbeat with his right foot onto a hollow wooden box with a built-in microphone. It resonated with a booming thud that sounded like a fist pounding against a coffin lid — from the inside. Meanwhile, his left foot kept the corresponding beat on a kick drum pedal which knocked against an upright washboard with a sharp "thwack." Robinson's ebony skin glowed with just a slight sheen of sweat next to the orange plaid fabric of his shirt. His tan Fedora and neatly creased slacks gave him the look of a long-lost uncle who wandered off into the woods on a weekend trip and never came back.

Red-eye was a former cattle rancher from Missouri. He

grew up scavenging scraps of musical wisdom like trea-
sured bits of driftwood floating along the Western banks of
the Mississippi River. Like most lifelong musicians, he'd
amassed a diverse set of skills for putting food on the table
between gigs. Although he was an accomplished player and
songwriter, he'd abandoned his dreams of the big time and
relinquished himself to infamous obscurity because he simply didn't have the heart to keep pimping himself out to an
uninterested populace.

Years earlier, a family tragedy had broken him emotionally — forcing him to sell his assets and move west after his
marriage fell apart. He found affinity among Denver's dis-
placed and despondent, and soon discovered that temporary
warmth and commiseration could be conjured by mixing his
music with some of the nastiest booze known to man.

Pablo sat down just in time to hear what he needed —
a song of betrayal and unrequited hope for reconciliation
written by a man who had been through the wringer more
than once.

As the tears fill up my lids
And the blood wells in my shoes
The evil that you done did
Gave me the blackest of the blues

Twist the knife, twist the knife
I miss my life but not my wife

I walk through the wat'ry night
Beside the ripplin' tide of moon
You're comin' back to me in time
With more salt for my wounds

Twist the knife, twist the knife
I miss my life but not my wife

I'll wait beneath the cuckoo clock
Inside our old bedroom
You'll sneak in without a knock
And be a-sealin' your own doom

Twist the knife, twist the knife
I miss my life but not my wife

Pablo let the music wash over him as he ordered three doubles of scotch. *Badger's Breath Whisky* was a notoriously harsh brand of hooch, revered for its high proof and for inspiring patently bad behavior. The first sip was like a kerosene punch to his throat, but he choked it down with a clench of his teeth and settled onto his seat like a head case onto a shrink's couch. Red-eye Robinson finished out a set and announced a short break, once he walked off the stage and set his eyes on his favorite spot at the other end of the bar, he noticed a familiar figure hunched over the wood in a wide-brimmed Stetson cowboy hat. "My god," he grumbled. "I thought I smelled something bad. Vasquez, you shit-talking' ditch weed toking fool. What the fuck?"

"Howdy Red-eye. Just thought I'd stop by and see if I could find a reason not to hang myself tonight."

"Oh no," he sighed. "Luna?"

"Yeah man. Sucks. Real bad." Pablo waited a few beats for the news to sink in and to garner the will to explain the circumstances. "It's not that we had a fight that was any worse than usual, I think something bad has happened to her, but I don't know for sure."

"Is those what I think they are? Double shots of *Badger's Breath*? Pablo, you know I can't drink that shit!"

"Damn straight, amigo — I know — but this is an emergency. C'mon man, please. Just one more time for me. I need it. I really need it."

Pablo and Red-eye went back decades. They started out playing music around the same time — slumming about the club circuit of the 70s and 80s, riding the nostalgic wave of the 90s and somehow finding relevance in the early part of another century. Through that time Red-eye learned to avoid *Badger's Breath* — for the most part — and to imbibe it with discretion under special circumstances only.

"You sorry-assed hangdogging sonofabitch." Red-eye always talked trash to Pablo because he could take it. "I don't see your ugly face for months and suddenly you come trudging in here asking me to fuck up a perfectly good night of music. You're a fuckin' prick, you know that?"

"How 'bout 'Baby of My Baby?'" Pablo knew his old pal had a soft spot for a wayward friend.

"God dammit." Red-eye gritted his teeth, contemplating an impending miasma inspired by a tale of his own woe. After a minute or so of staring at the bar top while grinding his molars together he spoke. "OK fine. You're welcome, asshole."

Red-eye Robinson grabbed a brimming glass of *Badger's Breath Scotch* and considered it for a moment before dumping it down his throat in one swift gulp. He slammed the glass down on the bar, snatched the other one from Pablo's hand and repeated the feat. He then wiped his mouth with his sleeve, turned without a word and headed back towards the stage. 'Baby of My Baby' was the saddest song he'd ever written, and now that he had half a dozen ounces of rotgut scotch in his belly — it was going to be rendered in a particularly crippling fashion. Red-eye had discovered decades ago that this particular spirit caused his vocal cords to temporarily loosen and expand into thick, steak-like slabs. This was caused by compounds that occur when the oils from the oak aging barrels bonded with the alcohol molecules to form phenolated carboxylic esters – known to have the same effect as honey. When he sang in a slow cadence after drinking it, his low, even vocal tone carried a timbre that agitated the aural nerve — causing the listener's brain to light up with activity. The onslaught was a five-prong neural saturation into the amygdala, the left thalamus, the hippocampus, the right occipital lobe and the left insula – the areas that register sadness.

He eased into a simple three/four timing, minimalist chord progression as his feet accompanied the melody with a shuffling waltz of a beat.

The day the baby of my baby
Drowned down in darkened hell
She went a-skippin' 'mong the daisies
And tripped and fell into the well.

As the first verse floated past his lips and into the ears of his peers, an invisible wave of sadness slowly surged across the room. It was as though each person present was kicked in the guts by a secret iron foot. Once doubled over, the strangling agony of the chorus kicked in while gasps of grief and sobs of sorrow began percolating throughout El Chapo.

Oh Lordy please save me
Help me find my little lady
You know I'm going plum crazy
About the baby of my baby

By now the notion of being the parent of an unbaptized child that was left unattended to fall to her doom and drown took on a deeply personal significance to each listener. The second verse into the repeat of the chorus inflicted another wave of misery-fortified guilt and remorse. The wailing

began and finally Pablo unleashed his anguish and joined in
with the blubbering.

Every soul from the town
Even the hounds sick with rabies
Looked all around across the grounds
For the gift my life had gave me

Oh Lordy please save me
Help me find my little lady
You know I'm going plum crazy
About the baby of my baby

By the time the final verse came around, El Chapo was
a cacophony of howling, lamenting grief — as some clung
to the bar like shipwrecked sailors to driftwood while others
flopped onto the floor in fits of flailing woe. Among them
was a wino named Buster. He drank only cheap red vino by
the pint glass — affectionately referred to as *Dago Red*. He
committed to his bawling like an inconsolable infant, and the
moment his wailing amplified to the resonant frequency of
100 decibels, every window in the joint shattered.

We found the baby of my baby
Stone dead cold and blue
You know the baby of my baby
Well she was my baby too

Oh Lordy please save me
Help me find my little lady
You know I'm going plum crazy
Without the baby of my baby

As Red-eye Robinson's final note of "Baby of My Baby"
rang out and faded away, the anguished-wracked patrons of
El Chapo convulsed with their residual sobs. Buster let out
one last whine of anguish and every half-full glass on the

bar burst into shards. Gradually, the mood lightened, folks straightened up in their chairs, brushed themselves off and regained their composure. Pablo wiped the tears from his eyes with one hand and the snot from his nose with the other, inhaled deeply and sighed out loud, "Thanks Red-eye. I needed that."

Chapter 26

Come Here

In the middle of a saliva-swapping mouth mash, Earl reached across his torso with his right hand to touch Cricket's left breast. She deftly unzipped her leather coat, shrugging it off and arching into his caress. Her nimble fingers found the hem of his beer-soaked shirt and yanked it upwards, "Damn, dude. You're stacked."

"I get a lot of core exercise."

Their shared levels of unnatural toxicity became neutralized into an alkaline writhe of passion and fumbling exploration. She reached down and found his aching erection. He had been manually fulfilling his sexual needs for many years now, so the feeling of another's hand around him was otherworldly — causing his nervous system to light up like a carousel. Cricket shimmied out of her black leather pants with deft wiggle, and Earl — for the first time ever in person — witnessed the breathtaking beauty of the nude female form. She was brave and reassuring. "It's ok. I've done this before."

"I haven't."

"I know, I can tell."

He was naked in front of a woman for the first time, and somehow, he was without the awkwardness that usually followed him around like a steppenwolf. Moonlight beamed through the window into Earl's apartment and lit up her ivory skin. Cricket yearned for physical passion but knowing her toxicity could maim any normal guy she abstained. On this night, however, she relished in the feeling of his manhood slowly entering her. They kissed again, beer breath and tequila drool swirling into a lather of lust — a wanton melding of saliva, sweat and triumph.

Never in all his years of whipping up escapist fantasies did he imagine that the woman of his daydreams would be perched atop him, as they humped in harmony on what used to be just another sofa of loneliness. He thrust up into her, finally understanding why men will do or say just about anything to experience the sublime bliss of lovemaking.

Her pink areolas arched upward, hardening into concentrated vortices of electricity. She rode up and down upon his lifetime of desire, her sweating haunches undulating with determination and purpose.

Cricket was about to climax, and as she reached the pinnacle of passion, so too did Earl. She gripped his ears, held on tight, and began a miasma of explosive pelvic contractions. Earl felt the unstoppable volcano rising through his vas deferens, into the shaft of his dick and ultimately into the pink, waiting grip of Cricket's sopping wet crotch.

She held him tight as they spasmed together and then collapsed into a steaming heap of crumpled clothing and sweating skin. She whispered into his ear. "Thank you, Earl.

That was fucking amazing."

The opposing polarities of one who could have anyone and one who could have no one had finally met, and the gyrating sphere of that attraction had alas, begun its revolution.

The post-orgasmic hypothalamus gland in Cricket's brain released generous jets of Oxytocin into her bloodstream. This chemistry activated her toxic salivary glands in a reaction that was complementary to a shot of tequila — causing them to release a compound more virulent than before. So, when she took a post-coital swill from her flask and spat a tiny squirt onto the wall behind the couch — just for the hell of it — the liquid began to eat through the paint with a sinister hiss.

Earl relished in a moment of clarity, as the reality of his circumstances flooded his awareness like a garden hose gushing into his eyeballs. In a matter of months, he had gone from a civically inept recluse whose only social recourse was silent drinking in the presence of other losers, to a man with power, purpose and the adoration of a gorgeous if not a tad bit crazy woman.

"My whole life I struggled to explain myself, until I finally decided it was easier to just keep my yap shut. Then, I discovered how to express myself by simply belching … I suppose I'm pushing my luck to try and communicate with sentences like everyone else."

"You'll never know unless you give it a shot. It's not like you're gonna say anything that surprises me after what we've been through."

"Before, I drank to numb myself and now I do it to exact justice on assholes. It's been a strange few months to say the least. It's just weird that in order to make things right I have to be half in the bag."

"I know how you feel. I can blind people with my tequila spit, but it comes with the price of being nearly incapable of intimacy without hurting someone when I don't want to. We had both better count our goddamn blessings. We can each understand, at last, what it's like to be normal by hanging out with another freak."

Earl pondered for a minute and then decided to give it a shot. "What if we fall in love?"

Cricket was ready. "What if that's already underway, huh cowboy? If you can't handle that shit, you'd better get the fuck out now. Your only other option is to buckle up and hang on with both hands. It's gonna be one helluva ride and aside from me and Pablo, you might not have any other travel companions." She took a swig from her flask. "I know for a fact that it sucks to go through life alone."

Earl cracked open a beer "Yep. Me too."

Chapter 27

A Sense of Impending Doom

Pablo wondered if he could muster the resolve to hide his heartbreak from his acolytes. He figured he could still fool Earl but with Cricket there was no way. He also knew it was simply a matter of time before these two freaks found each other, and the fact that the inevitable had already materialized was the sole piece of good news. "Fuck it," he muttered. "Honesty is the best policy."

He knocked on Earl's door holding a twelve pack of *Quasimodo Gold* and a bottle of Cricket's favorite tequila — the aptly named *Granny Slapper*. He slumped down on a chair across from Earl's couch and Cricket could see the pain in his face. She thought maybe using one of his wise cracks would cheer him up. "Jesus, Padre — you look like you got jacked in the ass by a barnyard donkey."

"Thanks kid, but please — just shut up and drink, will ya?" He tossed her the bottle of *Granny Slapper* as Earl tore into the cardboard case of *Quasimodo Gold* and pulled out a beer. "I have a terrible feeling in my guts that my worst of fears has come to pass. I think Luna has finally shit on me for the last time."

Cricket was glib. She had become accustomed to his defeatist exaggerations. "Oh, for crying out loud. What the fuck now?"

Earl became genuinely concerned as he took a pull of beer. "OK seriously though, what's going on?"

"I've warned both of you little shits about how dangerous EAR is, especially to people like us."

"So what?" Cricket was still unfazed. "We keep our heads on a swivel and try and keep a low profile. I mean, well, at least *I* do." She winked at Earl who was turning red behind his can of beer. "Which is more than I can say for this crazy bastard."

Pablo leered at Earl. "The fact that your belching ability pretty much prevents you from keeping a low profile is fine, because if things pan out the way I think they are going to then it doesn't matter and we're heading for all-out war."

Cricket got serious and sat down next to Earl. "Oh shit." She yanked the cork from the bottle and took a hit. "OK daddy-o. Lay it on us."

EAR is extremely dangerous to me and to those around me — deadly in fact, due to my past relationship with the head of the agency, Raul Geisel." Pablo took a deep breath and launched into an abridged history of the war of attrition between himself and the man who was once just a small-time music promoter.

Earl and Cricket listened with fine-tuned radar, relishing the moments of brilliantly executed humiliation while dreading what they ultimately meant. If Pablo's ego-crushing swats of smite were ever avenged by Geisel, the results would be extreme due to the compounded resentment which had built over time. If Geisel ever found Pablo, he would destroy the time-freezing troubadour and everyone around him.

Pablo's tone was grave. "If Luna went to Geisel and exposed me, she's already dead and he knows I'm still in Denver."

Cricket was mid-swig and did a spit take, sending a searing slick of tequila sailing across the room. "Oh, fuck me sideways, man. You've got to be kidding."

Earl knew he was in the path of danger headed Pablo's way. He also knew he owed the transformation of his character and his life to the guy, and he vowed to stand by him and reciprocate. "I got your back, Pablo. Fuck this Geisel guy and his EAR cronies." He took a swig of beer, swallowed and flexed out a belch that shook the walls. "Fuck their stupid vans and their weapons of sound and fuck the goddamn Gasser too — first and foremost."

Pablo and Cricket knew Earl was earnest but hearing him articulate with such bluster and conviction took them by surprise. Just as his belching ability was becoming more accurate and prolific, so too was his ability to explain what was on his mind and in his heart. He was living proof that sometimes enabling friends and copious amounts of beer can do a man good.

"We have to be careful, because once EAR picks up my scent, they will most likely enact martial law onto the city. They'll shake down, interrogate and incarcerate every band, bard, ballerina and balladeer in the greater metro area in order to find me."

Cricket spit again, this time deliberately — hitting the

Quasimodo Gold case. Her saliva hissed upon impact, and quickly melted a scar down the side of the box.

Pablo raised his eyebrows in amazement. "Melting stuff, now are we? Nice. *Very* nice."

Chapter 28

Sound the Alarm

The EAR agents who responded to the bout between The Gasser and The Belcher submitted reports of the unnatural incident that made Blatherskite giddy. The fact that his minions were acutely brainwashed meant they were incapable of making up stories of people with strange abilities. This also meant that, as birds of a feather flock together, chances were good that one of these freaks knew of Pablo Vasquez and his whereabouts.

After assessing the damage to his personnel vans, his urban terror gadgets and his men, Blatherskite held a general assembly of all agents and employees of EAR to issue an agency-wide order. Before taking the podium, he squirmed backstage at a small white table with a reflective glass top, chopping up two fat lines of MORE. His hand trembled as he inserted the double-barreled snort straw into his nostrils and aimed it at the dope rails on the table. He was furious and determined to sear the immediacy of the issue at hand into the grey matter of his minions. "I will rid will this city of these fucking freaks. I'll scribble out their stupid faces and names from the annals of history." He inhaled both lines in one hoggish, eyeball-bulging snort.

He quivered and shook his head from side to side in a rapid oscillation that would have given an inexperienced thrasher severe whiplash. "Pablo is goading them on, spreading pathogens of a deadly virus that must be burned out of the gene pool."

Blatherskite marched out onto the stage and stopped at the podium, its milk-white veneer blending perfectly with the ebony threads of his suit. The assembly hall was adjacent to the EAR tower, and featured a stage that was nothing more than a barren slate of fascism-inspired minimalism, with two thin white columns rising on either side to meet the towering ceiling and the EAR insignia centered above the podium, looming over Blatherskite like a victor's shield. The only animated element on the stage were the tiny fibers in the musculature of his face, which began to twitch with violent fervor as the MORE took hold. His flesh was nearly humming as his eyes strained forth from their sockets, his lips peeled back in a ghastly grimace and his jugular veins slithered up his neck like pulsating snakes. His head seemed to be a hologram, projected from a malfunctioning device that kept fast-forwarding the image and then stopping at arbitrary intervals to rewind. He was trembling at a rapid frequency marked by fits and starts as his brain cells strained to absorb MORE.

"Greetings my brethren of the Environmental Agency of Restrictions. We have among the good citizens of this fair city a scourge, an epidemic, a plague that has run amok. There are two men with severe gastronomic maladies who are muddling up the streets as they carry out their grievances against one another. Some of you have seen them firsthand and are aware of the danger that threatens our neighbors, our friends and our families. But we will not be daunted, nor shall we cower at the sight of these terrorists posing as self-expressionists. I WANT THOSE TWO MOTHERFUCKERS CAPTURED IMMEDIATELY!" His voice boomed about the assembly hall, the tonal frequency captivating his minions and snapping them into a state of undivided attention.

Blatherskite's head zig-zagged back and forth like he was indicating "no" at 1,000 miles per hour. A fine spray of spit was scattered forth into the air about his head like an aura of mouth mist. If he had dentures in his head they would have flown out, and the way he was grinding his teeth meant there was a good chance some bridgework was in his future.

"These vermin are spreading deadly pathogens with their guttural blasts and toxic vapors. They are part of an extremist movement to turn us all into barfing, shitting freaks." Blatherskite motioned to his assistants and the lights in the assembly hall went down as large 12' X 12' pictures of Earl Danners and Luther Fisk were projected side by side onto the back wall of the stage. The images were enhanced from cam footage from one of the EAR vans several nights prior. Each man was featured in all his glory. Earl was roaring out a mighty belch with the beer Cricket gave him clenched in one hand, looking like a fangless Mandrill Baboon about to strike. Meanwhile, Luther was shown squeezing out a toxic rush of rectal fumes, a grimace on his face like he had just stepped barefoot onto a sea urchin.

"You see these grotesque monsters? You see, my brethren? They are out there right now, polluting our city with their foul emissions. They hide indoors by day and scurry about at night like rats. They scamper from one filthy hole to another, infecting the rest of their kind with disease. DO YOU KNOW WHERE THESE RAT HOLES ARE? DO YOU?" The tiny beads of spittle mist were lit up like a halo as they scattered from Blatherskite's flailing head. "They are in taverns and bars, music halls and concert venues. They go to these shitholes to proliferate with their kind because music and singing are the same as belches and farts. It's just a bunch of hot air tainted with putrid pathogens that'll make your sweet mother puke up her lunch in your face."

The ranks of EAR agents, assembled in perfect rows 10 X 10, did not flinch at the image. Blatherskite's hypnotic screed had spun them into a transfixed state of singular focus upon their targets.

He continued his harangue "I want this city scoured for these two individuals and their accomplices." He motioned again to his assistants and the next set of slides pictured Pablo and Cricket. He pointed over his right shoulder "This man is their leader." It was a photo from the police car dash cam the night Pablo was teaching Earl to direct his belch bursts for maximum effect. "He is my mortal enemy, and yours as well. He is very dangerous and should be apprehended with extreme prejudice. He is known as Pablo Vasquez, but some call him The Soothsayer. If he tries to speak to you, cover your nose and ears." He motioned over his left shoulder. The image was from the EAR van dash cam — Cricket was helping Earl gather himself as the Gasser approached. "This little whore is their … well … she's a whore — and prostitution is illegal so arrest her on sight!"

The lights came up and Blatherskite gathered his composure enough to stop his head from nearly flying off his shoulders. "I am issuing a decree for the apprehension and capture of these four individuals by any and all means necessary. This is a civic emergency, and this department maintains the authority to enact martial law in the event of a terrorist threat. You will be deployed in ten teams of ten. Whichever teams succeed will be rewarded handsomely with unlimited amounts of MORE! Do you hear me, my brethren?!"

The EAR Headquarters assembly hall boomed with a resounding, synchronous roar from 100 brainwashed men. "YES SIR!"

Blatherskite pared down the orders for his troops into a convenient war chant, knowing that the cadence would etch the message into their exposed subconscious minds with permanence.

Hunt them down
Lock them up
Slit their throats
To fill our cups

They latched onto his chant and began repeating with vigor until the EAR Headquarters assembly hall was shaking at the foundation. To break their spell, snap them out of the trance and send them to their respective deployment stations, Blatherskite simply triggered the deployment drill alarm system with a button wired into the podium. As the roar cascaded down to an orderly murmur, he thought about his old friend Pablo, and how good it was going to feel to stomp his face into a bloody pulp.

As he sauntered off the stage, Blatherskite sung to himself with glee. "Oooh that was good. I think it's time for some MORE."

Chapter 29

Uneasy Fortifications

Earl was discovering that he was not fond of visits to Parental Planninghood. Once again, he found himself in the waiting room — this time at the Glendale location since the Capitol Hill branch was still being repaired after The Gasser's rampage. Cricket had missed her period, and they sat there fidgeting in unison — both in comparable states of panic. It was a few days after their pow-wow with Pablo and the compounding tension was palpable. "I'm ... I'm really sorry" Earl stammered.

"Oh, Jesus fuck, man — it ain't just on you." Cricket was fundamentally averse to victimhood. "We were both fucked up, you know? I figured it was OK to skip protection since you're half in the bag most of the time and you're probably shooting blanks anyways."

"Ummm, yeah ... good point ... I guess I never really thought about it that way." He absent-mindedly reached into his backpack, pulled out a beer, cracked it and took a swig. "What do you want to do?" Cricket found Earl's social virginity to be irresistibly charming. She had developed a deep-seeded disgust for men who wouldn't shut up about themselves and an acute mistrust for alpha types who thought they had all the answers. To her, Earl was a perfect yin/yang. Unconcerned with small talk yet blaring and sincere when speaking from the gut.

Cricket was similarly efficient, "We have to figure this shit out, pronto. If I'm not knocked up, I don't want to be."

For the time being they were both silent, Earl squinted internally at his freshly-upturned life while Cricket considered the pros and cons of motherhood versus abortion. Earl tried to imagine his life a few months prior. Aside from his menial job at the Denver Public Library, everything else had changed. His life seemed impossibly inevitable, as though the unlikely person he had become was always in there, waiting to find a way out.

Earl's newfound escape from self-doubt and fear had catapulted him into a world of danger, passion and bleary-eyed hangovers. He used to drink to become numb, now he had to guzzle beer in order to be effective — to fulfill a purpose. The fundamental dynamics of life had been flipped on him and he found himself staggering mentally and physically to adjust. He used to be silent, invisible and crippled by loneliness. Now he had volume, power and a female embrace he alone could endure. "Don't even question it." He thought aloud in a barely audible mumble. "Just go with it …"

Cricket jumped as he muttered. "Just go with what?" She was wracked with hair-trigger nerves and took a swig from her flask. "What the fuck do you mean, Earl? We don't even know what's going on yet."

"Yeah, uh sorry ... was just thinking I should go with my plan to go stock up on some more beer."

"OK sweetie. Hey, will you grab me another bottle of *Granny Slapper*? I'd hate to run out."

Meanwhile, west of Glendale near downtown, Luther Fisk was thinking about the noxious creation he had just dumped into his gastric cauldron. It was a rancid glop of sludge that was churning in his guts like green lava. He had harvested more sewage from the secret porthole adjacent to his workshop and mixed in some sauerkraut, a bundle of brown asparagus and a putrid tangle of spaghetti infested with more microbes than a head full of shit ropes on a white trustafarian. He rubbed his filthy fingers together and boasted to himself, "The surface area on a strand of spaghetti is more conducive to mold than an entire slice of soggy bread."

The Gasser's intestinal bacterial overgrowth had exacerbated his lactose intolerance — turning his body's inability to break down sugar into a prolific malady of methane fume production. Gallons of whole milk stored in the building's boiler room gave fluidity to his concoctions that he often topped off with sour prune juice, just for taste.

Luther had devised a way to extend his flatulence — which like urine and solid fecal matter — can simply run out. He began bottling his mixtures as field rations to fuel his bank robberies and pursuits of infanticide. He thought of the mustachioed bartenders in the hipster clubs across town with their moustache wax, dainty garnishes, hand-squeezed juices and imported liqueurs. "Craft cocktails, my ass," he grumbled.

Earl headed northwest from Parental Planninghood down Leetsdale Avenue. He was relieved to be able to slip away from an awkward situation. The discussion of female reproductive issues made him nervous due to his simple lack of experience or understanding. Apparently, there was a problem within a mysterious labyrinth of tubes, tunnels, organs and orifices and he may be the one responsible. There was immediate hope ahead, however — promised by the blinking neon letters that flashed in the happy cadence of L.I.Q.U.O.R.

Back at the clinic, Cricket was summoned to the exam room. She removed her leather jacket and tossed it onto a green chair. As she sat on the exam table the white butcher paper crinkled beneath her. The nurse's kind eyes and soft voice were a welcome distraction to what could be a worrisome ordeal. "Make yourself comfortable, sweetie. My name is Patty. Now tell me, what's going on?"

"I could have easily just pissed on one of those test kits you get at the drugstore, but I'm late *and* my guts hurt."

Patty's nose twitched, detecting acetate on her patient's breath. She was genuine yet professional. "Have you been drinking?"

"Yeah, well … a little bit. You see, I have to … as a protection mechanism."

"Really? How so.?

"Um, well …" Cricket wrung her hands together. "I believe there are certain properties of the agave plant that are beneficial to my system. That's why tequila is kind of like green tea to me."

"Oh my. Really? You drink tequila like it's green tea? That's absolutely dreadful. What's your brand?

"*Granny Slapper.*"

"Oh honey, if you're drinking that swill every day you've probably got an ulcer."

Patty gave Cricket a physical exam, a pap smear and administered tests for STDs and pregnancy. The physical revealed that Cricket was in excellent health. As she waited for the pregnancy test results, she pondered the walls that were adorned with framed diagrams of the female reproductive anatomy.

A few blocks east along Leetsdale Blvd, Earl was leaving Monaco Liquors with 750 mL of *Granny Slapper* Blanco and a twelve pack of *Quasimodo Gold*. Outside the store, the usual mix of predators were lurking about — a spare-changer in a black hoodie still-hunting by the front door, a thief in tattered Army fatigues pretending to tinker with a bicycle and a grifter in tan khakis and a pink polo shirt, fumbling with a gas can, performing the ol' "my car is stalled up the street and I just need a few bucks for fuel" routine.

It was a given that they were all in cahoots, and Earl's newfound confidence gave power to his stride — leading them to believe he had something worth taking. He had spotted the trio on the way into the store, and rather than wait for them to close in as he headed back up the road, he stopped on the sidewalk in front of the store and put down his backpack.

The panhandler was behind him to his left, the bicycle dude was directly to his right and the gas can guy stood dead ahead at 12:00. Earl reached down, grabbed a beer, cracked it with a *'ka-chok'* and slugged it down in one tilt. He sucked in a mouthful of air, swallowed hard and stepped back with his left foot. He planted firmly and then twisted his torso to the left to face his would-be assailant. The belch was a rapid-fire sequence of esophageal flaps that sounded like the chute of a cement truck dumping liquid concrete into a manhole. The blast hit the guy in the face — whipping his head back against the store window and knocking him out. Earl continued his expulsion, thrusting his left hip forward and torqueing his upper body clockwise which cast a circular belch wave that toppled the gas can man and sent the bicycle guy flailing over his hardware.

As he stepped over the second subject, a dumb stricken voice peeped upward from the pavement. "Who the fuck are you, man?"

Earl's answer was simple and succinct. "Bluuuuup"

A few minutes later Earl approached Parental Planninghood to the sound of screaming. He broke into a sprint and ran into the building which was immersed in an unmistakably foul stench. "Cricket," he called.

"Earl!" She had been praying that he would get his ass back from the liquor store already. "I'm in here, dammit. Hurry!" He yanked off his backpack, slammed another beer and with a quick "whuuuuuup" cleared away the Gasser's dark green smog so that he could see and breathe. He zeroed in on the exam room, sucked back more beer and belched the door straight out of the frame. It flew forward, hitting the Gasser in the back and knocking him down. The one-two punch-like impact made him fart off cue — sending the door flying upward into the ceiling tiles.

At the far end of the room, the Parental Planninghood nurse lay slumped at the feet of a near-fainting Cricket, who was struggling to breathe and maintain consciousness. Luckily, the unhinged door had brought fresh air into the tepid room. The Gasser had trapped Cricket in another quest to fulfill his fantasies. His rancor at having his plans thwarted once again was apparent as he rose from the floor slowly — growling like a ravenous badger with a fresh kill in sight. Earl tossed the bottle of *Granny Slapper* just above Luther's head of matted black hair. Cricket snatched it out of the air by the neck, yanked the cork out with her teeth and took a quick swig. "Drinking on the job, eh lassie? I'm going to have to teach you how to take me a little more seriously." He turned and aimed his ass at her, yanking down his slop-stained grey sweatpants for maximum exposure. Just before he gassed Cricket, she spat a caustic glob of toxic saliva directly onto his bunghole — singeing him like boiling water spilled onto an infant's skin.

"Aaaaaauuughhh you fucking bitch," he yelped – lurching back and grabbing his butt cheeks "You burned my goddamn asshole!" With that, he sunk to his knees and squeezed out a rancid fart that hurt far more than it relieved, causing him to screech again and crumple in anguish. Earl belched again, clearing away the newest plume of fumes. He ran in, scooped up Patty and bolted with Cricket back through the doorway.

"Goddamn you stupid fucking freaks" Luther screamed after them. "I'm gonna splatter you both sideways for this."

Out in the lobby, Cricket slowed down and grabbed Earl's arm. "Hold on, baby. Stop for a second." Earl halted, grasping Patty firmly in his arms.

"What is it? We need to get the hell out of here."

Cricket looked over her shoulder at the doorless exam room that was glowing green with billowing methane fumes and hissing with the Gasser's agony. "He's down. We should take that fucker out while we have the chance."

"Ok," Earl agreed. "Beer me." Not wanting to chance putting the nurse down and back in harm's way, Earl held Patty in his arms as Cricket cracked a beer, placed it upon his lips and steadily dumped it down his throat in unison with the upward tilt of his chin.

"Rrrrrruuuuuuuuuuuoooooouuuuuugghhhhp" the belch

was like a muffler-less old Buick speeding down a narrow hallway lined with corrugated steel. The blast knocked the exam room walls inward and shook the support beams loose. Before the roof caved in on them, they sprinted away from the collapsing building.

Three blocks to the south, the sound of sirens and the feeling of a cold can of beer rolling across her forehead awoke Patty. Earl and Cricket had stopped at Garland Park to assess her condition.

She looked up from the grass at the duo. "Thank you for getting me out of there. Bless you two."

Before passing out again she reached up with her right hand and cupped the left side of Cricket's face. "Sweetie," she whispered. "You're pregnant."

Chapter 30

Aural Assault

It was a Friday night and squads of manic EAR agents fanned out across Denver, descending onto independent music venues like excited riot cops celebrating an annual baton-a-thon. Blatherskite's brainwashing rally had whipped them all into a tunnel vision frenzy, and no juke joint, neighborhood haunt or loud, smelly hole in the wall was safe.

The front and side entrances of Laureate's Lounge were stormed by EAR agents. The staff, performers and patrons were tear gassed, tased and gunned down with wax bullets.

An EAR van screeched to a halt in front of Insurrection Cafe and agents poured out onto the Broadway and Ellsworth Avenue sidewalks, assuming a L-shaped attack formation. This place was the epicenter of cultural mojo in Denver — a floor-to-ceiling treasure trove of beatnik keepsakes and pop culture media. There were aisles of 10-foot tall bookshelves, entire walls of comic books, bulging racks of rare vinyl, a coffee bar, pinball machines, snack cakes, postcards, chess tables and an eclectic mix of art sprawled across every inch of exposed wall space.

The mush-minded EAR agents smashed the flyer-covered windows with hammer spikes and charged into the cafe. They set the bookshelves and comic book racks on fire, then the sprinkler system kicked in — creating mass confusion. In the music venue at the back of the store, the grinding screamo racket of *Black Eyeliner Shitty* had concealed the noise of the EAR agents bashing their way inside. Meanwhile in the front of the cafe, they were fanning out, zapping aisle dwellers and bludgeoning those unwilling to leave a pinball game that was in progress.

The owner, Jake, was mixing the band behind the sound booth in the far rear corner of the property. Once the sprinklers turned on, he checked his security monitors and saw the agents terrorizing the place. He leaped over the soundboard, ran across the dance floor and grabbed the mic stand from the singer's laced hand. He yelled into the wire dome of the microphone. "Hey buddies! Everyone get the fuck out NOW! We are under attack!" Knockers emerged from between two bookshelves, walking toward Jake rather than running away.

She whisked the red scarf from her bosom — revealing the hypnotizing humps and crippling cleavage of her chest. "They're here."

"Yeah I know! Don't do that to me, it ain't funny."

"Not these, dummy ... armed EAR agents. A van load of them just burst through the front windows!"

"Yeah no shit Nancy Drew. They're destroying my goddamn store!"

"Not without a fight." Knockers had the glint of bloodlust in her eye. "Follow me."

Jake hesitated for half a second and then followed. They ran down a smoldering aisle towards the front of the store as knockers ripped apart the snap away buttons on her red blouse and further revealed her mesmerizing breasts — barely kept harnessed by the lacework of her black satin bra. She stopped behind an EAR agent who was repeatedly zapping a chess player "Hey asshole," she shouted. He turned around and seized up at once, his neck locked in a sideways twitch and his eyes bulged outward as he stared down the canyon of her cleavage.

As the EAR agent stood there frozen stiff, Jake swung the cast-iron base of the mic stand like a battle axe and bludgeoned him upside the head — knocking him out cold. "That's right! Take that motherfucker" Jake screamed. The band had fled the stage, but their instruments along with the microphone were still plugged in. It sounded like an experimental noise/profanity act as Knockers and Jake vanquished one EAR agent after another to the accompaniment of Jake's cursing over electric guitar feedback blaring through the main speakers. It was almost like they accidentally invented a new type of musical performance art. Bait and Switch Authority Thug Bashing. Jake was practically singing into the mic like a metal crooner. Knockers would get an EAR agent's attention, the guy would freeze in a stupefied moment of duh-face gawking, Jake would bash his brain silly with the base of the mic stand and scream, "Take that motherfucker!" Talk about a one hit wonder.

The store and most of the inventory were spared from destruction thanks to the sprinkler system, yet the band had been rounded up along with every other artist, poet and reader on site and hauled off to holding facilities. Jake was eventually tased and thrown into the paddy wagon with the others. Knockers escaped unscathed, running topless down Broadway with her outward-facing open hands in front of her eyes to keep herself from being blinded by the uppercuts of her own bouncing tits.

A couple of miles to the northwest, El Chapo had also been raided. A squadron of EAR agents bombarded the bar during Red-eye Robinson's set. They detained him, his band, the bar staff and most of the patrons except for Buster, who had taken refuge in one of the ladies' room stalls.

Buster was a part-time sommelier and a full-time barfly. Years of pontificating about the nuanced notes of tart chardonnays and robust cabernets had numbed his passion for vinous treasures. Pandering to Denver's conceited elite left a sour taste in his mouth, and the vinegary zap of *Dago Red* was the perfect pairing. He savored cheap vino like an expert pastry chef who harbored a secret love for vending machine candy. He found affinity amid the mumbling regulars of El Chapo like a magpie finds its place along a high-wire line of its peers. He'd park his five-foot-five frame onto a barstool and sip cheap wine while running his hands through his grey hair and cursing his clientele. During the current commotion, he had managed to snatch his pint glass of *Dago Red* from the bar top and scurry to safety.

He huddled against the ancient grime of the tiled restroom wall, the aroma of a thousand cheap blowjobs rendered by filth-caked prostitutes rose to his nose and made his eyes begin to water. The EAR agents were intimidating their captives with mob mentality rhetoric. "You are being arrested, detained and charged for violation of the latest sound ordinance decree issued by the Environmental Agency of Restrictions. Participating in musical expression or appreciation of any kind is strictly forbidden until further notice." The looped recording blared repeatedly from the EAR van loudspeakers and into El Chapo through the windows — most of which had yet to be repaired. "You will be held without bail until you are arraigned for your crimes."

This blatant violation of his first amendment rights was deeply upsetting to Buster. Beneath his white eyebrows, within bright blue eyes, his heartache began to swell. The tears trickled down his weathered face and dripped into his drink, which he sipped at steadily as he trembled. The tannins in the *Dago Red* flowing through his mouth and throat caused his vocal cords to constrict like tightly-wound, tensely-coiled guitar strings. In turn, his moans of frustration and anger escalated into an intermittent high-pitched whine that was known to cause temporary hyperacusis; overstimulation of the nerve fibers in the cochlea causing hybrid sensations of maximal hearing which registers as extreme pain.

As his vocal frequency neared 100 decibels, the murky glass of the bathroom mirror rattled in its frame and then shattered into splinters and shards. He blubbered as he whined "You goddamn bastards. Why can't you fuckers just leave us alone … whuuuuuuh ... let us drink and enjoy our music in … wwwaaaaaauuugh … motherfucking peace!"

His whining reached 105 decibels and his drinking glass exploded into shrapnel — leaving dozens of tiny cuts across his face and palms. The shock and pain furthered his fugue. As he realized he was slipping into a dangerous loop of misery and self-mutilation, he burst from the bathroom sobbing — a wine and blood-covered spectacle bawling with a deafening wail. The Whine-o's crying was like ice picks into eardrums, and the ten armed EAR agents dropped their rifles and covered their ears while the patrons — hands already up in arrest mode — slapped their palms to their ears with a flinch and a knowing wince. Buster advanced toward them — a staggering disaster of blood, wine, drool and tears, "Goddamn you scum-sucking fascist EAR shitbags. I hate you all!" As he swore at them between clenched fists,

Red-eye Robinson cheered him on like a music fan watching his favorite rocker play a hit song. "Atta boy, Buster! Let those motherfuckers have it!"

The El Chapo patrons — streetwise miscreants that they were — saw the opportunity to escape and in seconds were scattering out the door in a dozen directions.

Chapter 31

Pros among Cons

A tight procession of EAR vans skidded to a synchronous halt in front of the Glendale branch of Parental Planninghood. The amped-up agents were responding to a police radio report of a building collapse involving loud rumblings and noxious fumes.

The Gasser was struggling to flee, but his escape was blocked by a partially collapsed ceiling that had trapped him in the exam room. His eyes were scorching from dust, his throat was caked with debris and his butthole was puckered shut from Cricket's searing spit. His resolve to avoid the authorities at all costs gave way to panic. When he heard the EAR vans pull up, he began to call out. "Please goddammit, please! Somebody help me!"

The EAR agents extracted The Gasser from the rubble, assessed that he was in stable condition and placed him under arrest. Their authority over all emergency situations in Denver and the surrounding area was welcomed by local law enforcement. The Glendale cops stood idly by and watched the show — content that they needn't concern themselves

LUKE SCHMALTZ

with physical exertion. The Gasser began bargaining at once. He already knew, from word on the street, that bounties were on the heads of himself, The Belcher and Cricket — and he vowed to save his skin by establishing leverage. "I want to talk to your boss. The head of EAR." He repeated his demand again and again. "I know about a couple of people he is looking for and I guarantee their delivery."

One hour later, The Gasser was in Blatherskite's private office in the penthouse level of EAR Headquarters. Sitting across from him — a pasty-skinned, bloodshot, pockmarked, trembling specter of a tweaked-out man chopped out two lines of MORE on a rectangular mirror that rattled upon the white marble desktop. The sound of the razorblade tapping at the glass echoed about like teeth chattering in an empty skull. "My men tell me" … he leaned forward and snorted "*sssssssskkkkknnnnnnfffff* … ahhhh … they tell me that you have some information that may interest me."

"Word around town is that you're looking for folks with, er, 'exceptional' abilities."

"Yeah, you could .... *sssssnnnrrrffff* … you could … *sssnnff, sssnnff, sssnnff* … you could say that."

"Well … I know of not one but two of them."

"Continue."

"I recently met some dude with a rude, rather destructive belching problem and some slinky little minx who likes to spit on, uhh … certain things."

"I'm looking for a big-mouthed pothead named Pablo Vasquez, some call him The Soothsayer. I'm betting that the girl knows him. If you can assist my agency with getting our hands on that little cunt, I might see to it that you are treated with leniency when it comes to levelling charges against you for destruction of private property and attempted murder. But first, my curiosity is brimming inside me like a bad case of botulism. I must know more about this fascinating gastrointestinal anomaly of yours. You are the one they call The Gasser, are you not?"

"How 'bout this, pasty face," he was beginning to see his way out. "I'll tell you all about it, and I'll deliver the bitch to your doorstep under a couple conditions."

Blatherskite sighed. "Oh, for fuck's sake, here we go."

"Grant me temporary immunity, outfit me with a vehicle and a few of your goons and chop me out a couple lines of that there go-fast."

10 minutes later the two men were whipping up a scheme with wide-eyed excitement, flapping their hands about frantically and blabbering over one another at levels just below screaming.

Chapter 32

Summon Your Allies

When Earl and Cricket returned to his place, they found a note on the door.

Hey kid, things are heating up. It's time to unite the BANE of this city or perish. I'll be back shortly.

Two hours later, the air was thick between the six figures huddled in the dim light of the apartment. Earl broke the silence, "hey everyone, this is Knockers. She's, well … she's … um, just don't stare at her tits, ok?" Pablo tipped his hat, careful not to gaze too deeply into her cleavage. He'd already known about her for some time and was silently thankful to have her among his friends.

She was quick to assert herself, "I hope somebody here has a goddamn plan, otherwise I'm leaving to go split some more EARs." Red-eye Robinson and The Whine-o nodded at Knockers in unison. "It's a pleasure to make your acquaintance," sang one. "Uuuhhh, hey — hi there," whimpered the other.

Cricket took a swig of *Granny Slapper*, spat towards the floor and watched her spit hiss into the grime-covered linoleum. She was indignant, "What the fuck are we supposed to do, Pablo? The city is under martial law, and we're all just sitting here in the crosshairs."

The Soothsayer remained calm, but just barely. "OK my friends, listen up. EAR has many tentacles that are groping and choking at this city in order to flush out one man. That man is me. The head of the Environmental Agency of Restrictions is Raul Geisel — otherwise known as Blatherskite. I am his sworn enemy, and he aims to arrest me, torture me and kill me. The recklessness of my past has caught up with me, and I have inadvertently put every Denver musician, artist, activist and freak with strange abilities in serious danger. The time for running and hiding is over. In order to survive, we must cut off the head of this shit-talking Shiva where it sits upon the shoulders of EAR. If we take out Blatherskite, we can break the spell he has cast over his minions. Most of them will simply morph back into marginally corrupt public servants and porn-addled gamer geeks rather than the Rocky Mountain Gestapo."

Pablo's benevolence had imbued Earl with intense loyalty to the man. "All I can say is thank you, Pablo. For everything you've done for me. I am ready for fucking war. BLUUUUUP!"

"Fuck an A," chirped Cricket.

"Amen, friend," crooned Red-eye Robinson.

"I'll be your cleavage beast," blurted Knockers.

"Oh, for crying out loud count me in too. Goddammit it all to holy hell … huuuurrrrmmmmmpphh," whimpered the Whine-o.

Pablo continued with gritty resolve. "Good. I'm glad everyone here is on board. Merely obstructing EAR as it goes about its daily business of shutting down venues, arresting artists and blasting people to holy hell with those sound guns is not going to cut it. We need to take these fuckers out one van at a time and if necessary, one brain-blitzed smack sniffer at a time. We will set out in three teams. Knockers, you'll be with me. Buster, you'll go with Red-eye and Earl, you're with Cricket. We'll use the abilities at our disposal to distract, to incapacitate and to immobilize. Plainly put, we're going to give EAR a covert, vigilante-style ass kicking. But first, we need to go shopping."

Chapter 33

Ring the Bell

Blatherskite nibbled on his fingertips as he considered his freshly-hatched alliance with The Gasser. "I shall accommodate your requests at once," he spat, and then summoned his newly canonized squadron of MORE-maddened cannibals by hitting a red button on his desk that was wired to the barracks level. There, the signal activated the hinges on an antique dinner bell that was installed in the hallway outside the quarters of the new elite rank.

When it began to ring, the Dinnermen burst through the door and trotted towards the stairwell in a neat, single file formation. Their navy blue coverall uniforms had been augmented with black chest plates that resembled body armor. The distinguishing upgrades also looked a bit like heavy-duty lobster bibs.

As they filed into the inner sanctum of the top level of EAR Headquarters, Blatherskite beamed with pride as he introduced his precious praetorians to The Gasser. "My new friend, I introduce to you an elite rank of EAR agents. Behold, The Dinnermen."

"Yes sir," they shouted in unison, their brains twitching and straining in anticipation of a generous dose of MORE.

"What you see before you, Mr. Gasser, is an A-list unit of agents who are — ahem — *unburdened* by common morality. Under my command these men can facilitate the acquisition of any person I wish to detain. These fellows are savages — and with their manpower at my disposal combined with your pungent abilities we shall acquire my targets as one succinct unit. But make no mistake, the slightest hint of foul play shall have you bearing witness to a whole new meaning of heartlessness."

"Really? You think I'm scared of this goon squad of brain-dead, cracked-out kooks? What are they going to do, hold me down and eat me alive or some shit? Hah!"

"If you wish, I can arrange for exactly that."

"Uh … OK man, really I'm just messin' with you. It's all good. Just tell me what the plan is and let's snort some more zoot and go get this stupid bitch."

"I will need to brief my men and administer their, uh, rations of proprietary performance enhancement."

"Is that what you're calling it? Jesus, you're more full of shit than I thought. Whatever, man — but while you're giving your little boys a narcotic brain bath, I really need something to eat."

"You'll find the mess hall and adjoined kitchen in the lower level of this building. Do not attempt to leave. You'll be shot before the door closes behind you."

The Dinnermen were lousy janitors. When cleaning up the slaughter that took place a few days prior, they simply swept up the remaining bits of skin, flesh, cartilage and bone and plopped them into a trash can in the corner of the room.

The Gasser's nose led him to the garbage pail of maggot-ridden gore, and when he discovered Luna's putrid remains, he gasped deep with glee like a spoiled brat on Christmas morning. The fact that Blatherskite, The Dinnermen and the rest of EAR were permanently geeked out on narcotics meant that the kitchen was severely neglected. In addition to decaying flesh, he discovered a rotting bundle of asparagus curling like a bouquet of severed purple fingers, lumps of bad broccoli that looked like frosty wads of cow shit and a tub of blue cheese dressing. He peeled back the lid and discovered that the preexisting lumps of moldy cheese had sprouted angry heads of green fuzz that smelled like an overused outhouse in 100 degree heat. While munching away with glee, he sat on a block of ice he found in the freezer, slowly reducing the swelling of his festering anus. "That venom coughing little cunt," he cursed between bites. "I'm going to shit right in her fucking face."

Chapter 34

Shopping for Deals

The Soothsayer, The Belcher, Cricket, Knockers, Red-eye Robinson and The Whine-o sauntered up to the main entrance of the Rocky Mountain Sports Castle at 10th and Broadway five minutes before closing time. Cricket went in first, took a swig of *Granny Slapper* from her flask and spat an expertly aimed wad of spit straight into the camera lens above the door. As the glass began to sizzle, she sprung atop the checkout counter and blurred the cameras pointing at the entrance and down at the cash registers with similar precision.

Pablo entered next, puffing on a lit joint. He stopped and inhaled as Cricket covered her nose and mouth. The two employees behind the counter were already stunned at the sight, yet the guy managed to squeak out, "excuse me sir… bu, but, but," while the woman managed to hit the panic button — alerting security. Pablo expected as much, and exhaled as the guards approached, one from the rear of the bottom floor by the gun shop and two from the inclined second floor walkway at 10 o'clock. He began to chant as he exhaled a thick thunderhead of pungent smoke.

144

"Life can be a joy when mortality is a sport,
We're just here for some toys so don't shit your shorts."

As the wave of pot fog overtook the clerks and security guards, they froze in place perplexed. The Belcher entered chugging a can of *Quasimodo Gold*. He stopped, swallowed, inhaled and belched a wide burst of wind that cleared the smoke so that Red-eye, The Whine-o and Knockers could enter and set about looting the store for supplies that were essential to their mission. Right on cue, the automatic doors locked behind them at the stroke of 7:00 PM.

The Soothsayer bellowed out directions to his comrades "Buster, wait for your cue. Earl, Cricket, Red-eye and Knockers — you all have your lists. Fill them fast."

The Whine-o sat on the checkout counter with his bottle of *Dago Red*, took a huge swallow, slumped over and let the melancholy take over. Cricket's first score in the guns and ammo department were five pairs of target practice earmuffs. She put one set on and tossed a set to Pablo, Earl, Red-eye and Knockers. The five of them scurried off in different directions in search of walkie talkies, scuba gear, an extreme sports camera harness, GPS location gear, grenades, handguns, rifles and ammunition.

As the staff of the Rocky Mountain Sports Castle were about to reanimate, The Whine-o had already begun sniffling — reliving his lifelong miseries on cue like a seasoned method actor. He pounded the countertop in emotional anguish as he took another deep swig. Just as the staff began to stir, he let out a sharp whine at 100 decibels that hit every exposed eardrum aside from his own like a hot harpoon of sound. "Aaaaaauuuuggggh goooooddammiiiiit I didn't waaaaant to eeeeeven dooooooo thiiiiiis" he sobbed. The guards and clerks recoiled in pain, wincing their eyes shut and covering their heads. Buster leaned over mid-blubber and hit the *NO SALE* button on the register, pulling out twenties and hundreds as the gang reassembled in the lobby.

Earl took another can of *Quasimodo Gold* from his backpack, cracked it and downed half. He reared back, inhaled and then lurched forward — launching a gust of gut wind that shattered the front plate glass window facing 10th Street.

The silent alarm had long since alerted the authorities. But by the time the cop cars and EAR vans came screeching up, all that was left was a blown out storefront that held just a slight whiff of beer foam, dope smoke and cask-aged sadness.

As they made their escape, the irony was not lost on Pablo. "All these years of refusing to become a criminal and for what? Maybe the cranky ol' bitch was right after all."

Chapter 35

Spies Like Us

Earl and Cricket obscured themselves from the streetlights beneath the jagged shadows of the "Lao Tzu" sculpture outside of the Denver Art Museum. They were on the north side of the building, just a block or so from Earl's former place of employment — he had recently decided that going back was pointless. Just to the west — across Bannock Street on the south side of 14th, the EAR Headquarters building rose ominous into the moonlight like a giant concrete butt plug. The zeal with which Blatherskite carried on within even made the building seem to vibrate from time to time.

Cricket applied her streetwise expertise to their surveillance, "Just from looks alone I'd say breaking into that place will make one hell of a racket. We need to find the garage entrance to where they park their vans and sneak in that way." Earl was riveted by her unflinching resolve to commit multiple felonies and risk the consequences of capture. He had long since disciplined himself to never blatantly stare at a woman, yet he could not help but steal darting glances while they planned the evening's infiltration. Brief as they were, she could feel his looks. Smiling inwardly, she decided to catch him by surprise. "Hey baby, next time I catch you checking me out I'm going to yank down your jeans and blow you on the spot."

Earl's jaw went slack as his face flushed red. "Damn." He managed, clearing his throat. "That obvious, eh? I'm trying to stay focused, I swear. It's just that I'm … that … I'm …"

"It's OK sugar. I'm crazy about you, too." She slowly swayed forward from beneath a ribbon of shadow. The moon lit the ivory lines of her neck and porcelain curves of her face into a whitish radiance that beamed softly into Earl's eyeballs and upwards past the arms of Lao Tzu. Her lips lightly touched his, then gradually eased into place with increasing pressure, wetness and warmth. As they opened to let him in, her tongue met his with swipes of fiery saliva that would have seared any normal man. But, as usual, Earl was so tempered to toxicity that the warm caress of tequila — aside from making the front of his jeans bulge — gave him the sudden craving for a fresh gush of beer. They writhed in mouth-mashing ecstasy for a few more moments and at last pulled apart with a light smack. "Sorry champ." She was coy. "Now that I know what I've been missin', I gotta make up for lost kissin'."

"Kiss away … go right ahead, any god damned time you want is fine with me. Except … well, for now we better stop screwing around and get back to work."

"Good call, daddy-o."

They headed southwest through the museum campus towards the rear of the EAR Headquarters building at 14th and Bannock. Cricket was back down to brass tacks, "It's near midnight — right around now is when the vans get deployed to some nuisance in the area to shut down events and arrest people. When the door opens and they drive out, we can slip in and stow the GPS transmitters."

Around 12:10 AM, the sub-level garage door roared open and two vans came screeching out as though they were fleeing some unseen menace. "Jesus Christ," gasped Cricket. "Those assholes drive like they're fucking high."

They ran down the slanted driveway and slid under the door just before it slammed shut. The garage was a long rectangular concrete corridor with a middle aisle and rows perpendicular parking spaces lining each wall — 10 of which were occupied by EAR vans. The entrance gave way to a wide lane that led straight to the double door entrance to the basement level of the EAR Headquarters building. The entire hall was bathed in a yellowish hue from the overhead LED lights and the place stunk of motor oil, addiction and death. "Pablo said to tag the vehicles closest to the entrance" Earl recalled with a whisper.

"Copy that." They hid GPS transmitters within the back wheel wells of each EAR van — securing the units with generous amounts of black duct tape. As they finished the last placement, they were hit with the realization that they were temporarily trapped. Cricket became suddenly uneasy "Man I really want to get out of here right now. This place gives me the creeps." She crossed her arms and ran her hands up and down her leather sleeves. "I wish I could spit on the door frame mounting brackets to weaken them and you could belch-blast us out of here."

"That would work, but they'd know someone was in here and probably find all of the GPS trackers. It's OK. Those vans have to come back at some point, right?"

"I know, baby. Just wishful thinking."

149

They crouched together in the shadow next to the garage entrance. The corridor was an echo chamber of sorts, and exaggerated small sounds into large noises. Just beyond the double doors at the other end of the garage, they could tell that some sort of activity was underway. Someone or something was in there making racket as though it was rummaging through boxes, packaging and contents. Cricket was wary yet amused. "What the hell is that?"

"I don't know. But it sounds like a wild animal rooting through the goddamn garbage."

The rustling continued for a few more minutes, then gradually died down. Cricket was careful to whisper in the lowest register possible. "Jesus, look at this place. Those vans are like modern Gestapo machines — built to wreck shit, fuck people up and haul them to jail. Taxpayer funded, no less."

"Pretty intense. No wonder Pablo is enemies with these people. This place is like … the anti-Pablo or something."

Cricket nodded, then pivoted. "Do you ever have those moments that seem to be outside of time?"

"What, you mean like a Pablo-inflicted dope-freeze moment?" Earl quipped, half kidding.

"No silly, I mean when you get a second to stop and step aside from the momentum of life and observe what the fuck is actually going on. When you get a minute to look at your situation and wonder how the hell you even got there in the first place." Her eyes darted about — inspired by mischief while scanning for signs of danger.

"Hell yeah. I've had a few of those lately." Earl allowed himself an involuntary smile. "It's like — I can't believe everything that's changed for me in such a short time." He half-consciously reached into his backpack for a beer.

Cricket adored the change in Earl's face on the rare occasion when it lit up. "You should smile more." Again, her words had a physical effect on him, and he involuntarily cracked open the beer. The echo of the snapping aluminum raced down the length of the corridor and back again, jolting them both back into the moment.

They tensed, waited a few beats and then slowly exhaled — doing their best not to laugh out loud. Cricket pulled out her flask and unscrewed the lid. "I'll drink to that."

As Earl finished his beer Cricket stood up and extended her hand. "Don't you dare leave that fucking can behind." She barely mouthed the words.

"I know, I know." He whispered. He returned the empty can to his backpack and took her hand as he got up.

Cricket led him down the lane of EAR vans past the first occupied row and back into the shadows between vehicles. She brushed his blonde bangs out of his face and smiled into his fierce blue eyes. "Shhhhhhh."

Their kissing reignited the heat that had grown between them outside under the sculpture. Cricket wiggled out of her black leather jacket and pulled the white T-shirt up over her pale, round breasts — both popping upward and outward like miniature pyramids of flesh. Earl placed his mouth on her right nipple and caressed it with his tongue in slow circles, then moved to the left, kissing his way across her chest. She worked away at his belt, fumbling to free his pulsing dick that was reaching upward, aching for warmth. "Oh fuck," he gasped. "I can't believe —"

"Shush baby … I'm going to teach you the art of the quickie. This will make the wait fly by, trust me." She unzipped her black leather pants and pulled them down to

151

the tops of her motorcycle boots, followed by her lacy white panties. "Leave everything on. This is no time to be fucking around with shoes." She turned 180 degrees, presenting her firm buttocks towards Earl. He moved in close as she splayed her left hand forward onto an EAR van for balance and reached between her legs with her right hand to guide him in. Earl entered her with a slow, gradual and firm thrust forward. The wave of pleasure radiated throughout his body and made him grit his teeth so that he would not moan with abandon as he wrapped his arms around her torso. They eased into a quiet, steady rhythm as Cricket's ecstasy quickly elevated, and she began careening towards a climax. She was clenching her face in order to remain quiet with such intention that tears began streaming down her face. The visceral excitement of fucking in a place that could potentially get them killed was an inexplicable turn on. Earl was close to climaxing and she could tell by the fact that his whole body was like a clenched knot of muscle. "Don't pull out, baby. Give it all to me," she gasped. Earl came with a series of lovingly if not violent thrusts — the rocking motion of their conjoined bodies caused a tear to fly from Cricket's chin. It hit the dusty concrete and hissed with a tiny sizzle as her pelvis and thighs contacted in a quick series of orgasmic spasms that made bouquets of sparks explode behind her clenched eyelids.

They gradually composed themselves, pulled apart gently and re-affixed their clothing. "Holy fuckballs," Cricket whispered jokingly. "You're crazy, man."

Earl decided to go with it. "Sorry," he mouthed the words. "I don't know what came over me."

A short while later the garage door jolted into motion and opened as the EAR vans returned. The disembarking agents were jonesing so bad for MORE, they rushed into the building and made no attempt to assess the security of the garage. The two slightly intoxicated, love-crazed intruders stole away undetected.

Chapter 36

Urban Assault

After a sufficient night's sleep, the three teams met at Pablo's place for debriefing. "This is Headquarters. Got it, troops? It's sub-level, like a bunker, so we'll stay off the radar for longer. If it gets compromised, switch to Plan B — which is to meet at Earl's place and Plan C is to go to Red-eye's house. OK?"

A collective murmur rumbled among the ragtag band of fuckups. Pablo was no drill sergeant, and he countered with a preliminary initiative to fortify his unflinching friends. "While we're waiting for dusk, we should take that loot Buster snagged from the Sports Castle and mosey on over to Astronaut Liquors for provisions. Some *Quasimodo Gold* for Earl, a few flasks worth of *Granny Slapper* for Cricket, a couple boxes of *Dago Red* for Buster and — even though you don't want it — perhaps just a few pints of *Badger's Breath* for Red-eye. Whaddaya say?"

The idea seemed to perk up the gang's spirits a bit, except for Knockers. "What about me, motherfucker? You know I don't respond to booze like these assholes."

"Don't worry, sweetness. There's a boutique on Colfax just a couple blocks down. While these three schlubs are trying to keep up with Cricket, we can see about getting you fitted with a nice new lacy pink maximum cleavage bustier, OK?"

"That's more like it, pothead."

"Yeah, speaking of which, I need provisions myself — and watch it, Charro, or the next joint I smoke is getting exhaled straight down your catatonia canyon. We can have a full-on gawk-off." The moment of mirth was just what the gang needed to ease the tension. A collective chuckle erupted, and Earl accidentally let loose a pent up laugh-belch that shook the building's foundation.

"Jesus Christ Earl," swore Pablo. "When are you going to give up that foul swill and just start shooting your enemies like a real man?"

"Whatever you jackass" Earl was getting better at talking shit. "You're the one who turned me onto this bilge in the first place."

"You're welcome."

"How 'bout I thank you again by taking what's left of your guitar over here and smashing it across your damn face."

"Ouch. Atta boy, Earl."

The wisecracks fizzled out quickly as Pablo went from deadpan to dead serious. "OK people — anyways — today is Friday. That means tonight EAR will be making another sweep and shutting down any and all clubs that still haven't gotten the hint that exhibitionism is being executed. The most probable targets will be The Joker, Layman's Lair and the Sin Sack.

Earl, you and Cricket should take The Joker. It's time you made a triumphant return — maybe apologize for all the damage you did last time."

"Uuuulp."

"Red-eye, you and Buster stake out Layman's — it's smells almost as bad in there as El Chapo so you two will be right at home."

"Finger-pickin' good."

"Knockers and I will deal with the Sin Sack. I've heard they are lenient on enforcing the Colorado Clean Indoor Air Act and plus — there's burlesque show in there tonight and Knockers needs to show those bitches how it's done.

"Fuck an a right!"

Two hours after nightfall, Pablo and Knockers took a table towards the back of the room in the venue hall at the Sin Sack. The place was a time capsule of early 20th Century kitsch — part New Orleans brothel and part circus tent sideshow cabaret. Ceiling-to-floor ruby red curtains lined the walls in velvet ripples. The stage was framed in an ornate latticework of garlands and vines while antique fixtures and furniture created the perfect setting for an old-time, classy display of tits and ass.

Frisky Risqué was a burlesque troupe that had been captivating throngs of gay men, masculine women, empowered girly-girls and their sheepish boyfriends for the better part of two decades. As a steadfast fixture of the Denver entertainment scene, they vowed to proudly display their art regardless of the imminent danger of EAR. Their director and premier performer — Tushie Swayswiftly — began the night with a proclamation: "If the powers that be condemn the female form to be repulsive and a crime to freely flaunt, then I pledge to be a scantily-clad, tassel-twirling, ass-shaking, law-breaking bitch until the day I die. They can have my satin gloves and feather boa when they pry them from my cold, dead, immaculately manicured fingers!"

The first act commenced in a cascade of lounge, Lambada and lingerie. The whims and wiles were lost on Pablo and Knockers and they feigned fascination, waiting for the GPS receiver to buzz them into action. Intermission was scheduled for 11:15 but on Tushie Swayswiftly time that meant 11:45, give or take. At 11:43 Pablo's GPS receiver lit up. Knockers saw his glance and finished her beer. The EAR van had quickly sped from 14th and Bannock and was already barreling down Broadway towards the Sin Sack. Their position just south of Virginia Avenue meant big trouble in very little time.

Pablo had a split second flashback to his guerilla antics of a bygone era. He silently cursed away the sentiment, refocusing on the mission at hand. "OK sweet tits, you're up."

Knockers couldn't wait to strut her stuff. "Copy that, padre."

Pablo twisted both ends of a freshly-rolled joint and placed it between his lips with a wink. He took off his trademark wide-brim Stetson and placed it on the table, as it would have been a dead giveaway to EAR agents. As Tushie Swayswiftly introduced the last act before intermission, Knockers made her way backstage and waited. As Tushie ambled into the green room Knockers cut her off. "Hola mamacita, I know I'm not a featured act, but our friends EAR are going to storm through here any minute and start busting heads. I've got a friend out in the audience, and we are planning a little surprise for the bastards." She pulled down her purple scarf, revealing the magnificent magnetism of her bosom framed in pink lace. Even Tushie Swayswifty — who'd seen a million miles of lace-laden cleavage in her time — was taken by surprise at her own fascination. Normally a nonstop fidgeter, she halted involuntarily in a moment of suspended animation. Knocker snapped her out of it with a light slap on the cheek. "Get your all of your bitches backstage. We're going to trap these assholes and disable their entire assault team with temporary paralysis. When I give you the signal, that means it's time for the second act."

Tushie was reticent. "But the customers … our fans, what about —"

"Bitch, please!" Knocker quipped with a jiggle. "They'll be fine. Even the creepy ones. Now go announce intermission and get the fuck back here!"

The EAR vans pulled up as though they were the fire department and the place was ablaze. The agents clambered onto the cement and stormed into the club, knocking over patrons, shouting orders that everyone was under arrest and specifically hunting for burlesque performers in skimpy lingerie.

The stage was lit with a lone spotlight — an intense blue beam hinting at the audience that the best was yet to come. Knockers stepped into the cool column of hue and nodded towards the back. Pablo held Tushie's wireless mic he'd grabbed from the stage in front of his face which he further obscured with wisps of his long brown hair. The audience became subdued as armed EAR agents made their way around the tables toward the stage. The lead agent fondled his weapon as did the others. He began barking orders. "Put your hands u —." He was cut short by a low growl.

"Welcome to the peepshow, ye agents of EAR
But now it's a freak show and the stars are all here"

A momentary diversion was all Knockers needed. She whipped away her scarf and the glow from her lace-encased bosom seized the eyeballs and the loins of every man in the room. Their minds all began to blur as the blood in their skulls rushed down their torsos into their dicks and they all began to lean forward. Her enchantments seemed to have less of an effect on the EAR agents, although every man in the audience was gawking. "OK you peeping weasels, I got more for you suckers." She pulled down the front of new bustier and exposed her perfectly round rose-tinted areolas — each arching outwards and up, rising concentrically to apex columns of erectile tissue. Her nipples were power vortices that shot mesmeric beams of stupefaction into the hypothalamus of every onlooking brain.

Pablo flicked his lighter and noticed the agents were still creeping forth ever so slowly. It was just as he thought — the MORE-saturated brains of the EAR agents were going to need extra influence to be sufficiently subdued. Pablo toked on his joint and inhaled as he swaggered past them. He stepped onto the stage and was careful not to look at Knockers' chest. He moved beside her, into the beam of light and exhaled a gale of THC-laced poesy that washed across every face in the club.

"Gawk yourselves an eyeful
You geeked out virgin thugs
Nearest you'll get to insightful
Or a set of magnetic jugs"

Knockers wrapped her scarf around her ears and mouth to avoid the paralysis of Pablo's toking poetry — leaving her bosom blaring stark and loud. Involuntary guttural moans erupted from a few of the more excitable patrons as they uncontrollably came in their pants.

"Sleeping on the job
Is for the lazy and the wrong
And these pills will keep you hazy
Like the long fog of a bong"

Invariably, every maw in the place was hanging agape. Knockers flounced among the crowd, popping a fast-dissolving Rohypnol tab into each EAR agent's mouth.

"Well will you look that?" Pablo mused. "A perfect portrait of modern man. A bunch of drooling, speechless idiots with guns, hard-ons and not a fucking clue as to what the hell is going on."

As the Sin Sack patrons were beginning to regain awareness and retreat from the club in utter confusion, the EAR agents were slipping from one stupor to another. Knockers turned back towards the stage and shrieked "OK Tushie! Come get these motherfuckers!" The entire cast of the Frisky Risqué Burlesque Troupe charged from the backstage wings into the club, screaming and flailing in a furious throng of wigs, leotards, lingerie, satin, silk and sequins. They descended upon the EAR agents, pummeling them into piles of bruised goo with their high heels and pumps. "Don't forget the vans outside!" Knockers yelled.

"Come on, bitches!" Tushie boomed, and the evening's talent — pissed as hell that their show was cut short — followed her outside to ransack EAR's deployment of urban terror machines. The dazed staff and patrons of the Sin Sack stood in awe as what looked like a gang of brothel workers in skimpy attire flattened the tires, bashed in the headlights and smashed the windows of two large, unattended armored vehicles.

Inside, Knockers climbed back onto the stage, pulling the double F cups of her bustier back up into place. Pablo stood there motionless, the joint between his lips slowly burning towards his beard. She slapped him across the face to snap him out of it and the roach went flying. "I'll catch you peeking every time, motherfucker."

"Sorry, you crazy broad. You turned around too fast and I couldn't help it."

"No one can."

Chapter 37

The Wail in the Wake

Red-eye Robinson and The Whine-o headed east from Pablo's place like two poachers setting off into the woods. Red-eye had a pint of *Badger's Breath* swishing in the inside pocket of his plaid suit jacket and Buster was comforted by the weight of a box of *Dago Red* tugging at the straps of his backpack. Unlike Buster, carrying BANE-inducing booze around made Red-eye anxious. He regretted making rooms full of people inconsolably sad — especially Buster — whose deafening whine always made things worse.

They approached the Layman's Lair with the swagger of skid row regulars. From within the bar wafted the tepid stench of east Colfax – an aroma like a midsummer music festival outhouse brimming with excrement, bedazzled with flies and adorned with the charms of long-abandoned undies. What was usually a hive abuzz with riff-raff, banter and bluster was instead, a somber gathering beset by the heavy air of mourning.

Jimmy Jiggs was a staple in the Denver music community, especially in the punk scene — a rag-tag allegiance of emotional juveniles, savant idealists and criminal basket cases. His untimely death struck a particularly sour note in the hearts of an already troubled lot. Jimmy was a legendary guitarist notorious for lightning-fast leads played blindly from behind a mop of sweaty brown hair. His overtures defied every stricture of music theory and were unanimously regarded as "bitchin, dude."

Jimmy was killed a week prior at the Layman's Lair during an EAR raid. His band — Beelzebunghole – was a wild sonic dervish that was the essence of the unbridled mojo of the Denver underground. When the EAR agents stormed the Layman's Lair demanding silence and compliance, Jimmy kept on playing — leaping off the stage onto the dance floor, jigging his way over to a stool which he used to amble onto the bar top — all without missing a note.

Beelzebunghole was playing one of their most beloved tunes, and Jimmy would be damned if "Throw Rock at the Cops" was going to be interrupted by a bunch of civic recruits so fresh they had yet to shoot an unarmed civilian. The Layman's Lair was raided under the auspices of having exceeded the decibel limit which had recently been lowered to 40 — hardly enough volume to hear a scream over the pop of a snare drum. Jiggs was a notorious rabble-rouser, and unless he was unleashing dissonant six-string mayhem to a bar full of staggering drunks — he somehow seemed out of place.

Throw Rocks at the Cops by Jimmy Jiggs and Beelzebunghole

Throw rocks at the cops
Throw rocks at the cops
When the hammer drops
You just can't stop

They're gonna shut you down
And lock you up
Throw rocks at the cops

Do jigs on the pigs
Do jigs on the pigs
When they pull the plug
Gobble all your drugs
The lugs are all thugs
So it's time to cut the rug
Do jigs on the pigs

Excrete on the heat
Excrete on the heat
When they point their guns
And you get the runs
Just shit in your hands
And throw it at the man
Excrete on the heat

When the band refused to quit playing, the crowd was emboldened and joined in on the song's breakdown — a relentless chant of the opening phrase "throw rocks at the cops." The EAR agents considered the collective gesture to be an overt threat. The squad leader aimed his taser at chest level, pulled the trigger and squeezed 50,000 volts directly into Jimmy's chest. The electric zapping ignited the 101 proof *Badger's Breath Whisky* soaked into his shirt and hair. He cramped into spasms and burst into flames in the same moment, clutching his guitar like it was a rifle and he a soldier — momentarily freeze-framed as his foot hit the proverbial landmine. Whether he died of a heart attack, severe burns or both had yet to be determined.

The gallery of mourners at the wake of Jimmy Jiggs was a snapshot of the collective underground mindset. An assemblage of seething personalities who were maimed by heart-break, confounded by circumstance and profoundly pissed off. The emotional barometer swelled up considerably when Red-eye Robinson and Buster walked in. Jimmy Jiggs was a longtime friend and one of Red-eye's unofficial musical acolytes. Red-eye had heard the bad news through the grape-vine just after the raid at El Chapo went down, so he took the Layman's Lair assignment as a matter a personal interest and paternal obligation.

Red-eye took the pulse of the place and read it as an undercurrent of suicidal depression and homicidal rage. He nudged Buster and muttered, "You better drink up, Whine-o."

"I have my doubts as to how much, if any, *Dago Red* they keep on hand here. Good thing I came prepared." The Whine-o was a homing beacon for drama and a magnet for misery. In any setting, the most emotionally unstable and mentally feeble people would gravitate towards him in search of a kindred spirit. Like most men he was sentimen-tal, yet he was set apart by the fact that he had no prob-lem showing that he gave a damn. On any given evening he could be found holding court with the downtrodden, the abused and the unjustly shit upon. In an effort to mitigate the fallout from his high-pitched BANE, he relegated himself to drinking measured amounts in loud places while deliber-ately muffling his deafening whine by holding his lips shut and breathing through his nose. This made him an excellent listener, as any attempt to contribute to a litany of complaints from a new friend would give him away as a true freak while adding to their misery.

Microphones and guitars were set up in the corner stage of the Layman's Lair. The structure was an ankle twisting trap of rotted wood positioned diagonally towards a "U" shaped bar that resembled a corral for the bartenders who were milling about like recently-tranquilized livestock. The walls were plastered with vintage velvet paintings of unrelated theme — lions, ballet dancers, caballeros in sombreros and Elvis. At least three or four stickers from every local band to have strummed a note in the place over the last 20 years adorned every surface — the bar top, the jukebox, the bathroom walls, the front door, the back door and the street-facing windows. Every rocker, metalhead, thrasher and noise junkie in Denver seemed to be in attendance. Anyone present who so desired would be given at chance at the microphone to give Jimmy Jiggs a proper send-off.

Red-eye and Buster sat through a blubbering procession of leather-clad, flannel-draped sorrow as they steadily juiced up for a showdown. The fact that people were playing songs and reciting poetry through amplified means meant that the Layman's Lair was asking for more trouble by violating the new noise ordinance. Clearly, no one gave a shit.

Red-eye's GPS receiver buzzed to life at 12:15 AM, and it showed two EAR vans had been dispatched and were heading east on Colfax towards the Layman's Lair. He was considered musical royalty in Denver, and as a young punk was finishing a teary-eyed tribute to Jiggs, Red-eye approached the stage and extended his hand. "Nicely done, young man. May I borrow your fiddle for a few minutes?"

Starstruck, the young man took Red-eye's hand, grasped it and eagerly handed over his acoustic guitar. Red eye took the stage and faced the audience. Most in attendance knew who he was and were wondering if he was going to talk, or better yet, play a song. "Good evening my friends," he began. "I'd like to talk to y'all at length about Jimmy Jiggs, but I'm afraid there's not much time." He tuned the guitar as he continued, "You see, in about 90 seconds a deployment of EAR agents are going to come screeching up in a couple of those black vans and busting through that front door. DO NOT PANIC, my brothers and sisters." After raising his voice, he eased back down to the warm, reassuring, honey-dipped tone he was always known for. "My colleague Buster over here and I have a sonic ambush waiting for them. All you fine folks have to do when that door open up is cover your ears, and we will do the rest."

Red-eye pulled out his bottle of Bader's Breath from the inside pocket of his red plaid jacket, slugged down in one chug and winked at the bartender. "Sorry. I know that's wrong, but I'm about to make it right." He launched into "Baby of My Baby" after drinking scotch for the second time in a week.

"The day the baby of my baby
Drowned down in darkened hell
She went a-skippin' 'mong the daisies
And tripped and fell into the well."

"Cover your ears, children," Red-eye warned again. "Here they come." Everyone in the bar complied except for Buster — who needed the sonic sorrow to induce his own. The EAR agents burst into what appeared to be a gathering of perpetrators who had already surrendered. The squadron fanned out into the bar to get a bead on the bartenders, any behind-the-wood weapons and of course, Red-eye Robinson.

"Every soul from the town
Even the hounds sick with rabies
Looked all around across the grounds
For the gift my life had gave me"

The EAR agents, despite their emotional insulation from copious amounts of MORE, were struck by the sadness of Red-eye's music — conveyed by a tonal quality they had never heard before. By the time the chorus was coming around, most were trembling on the verge of a psychological breakdown. The Whine-o was drinking it in as well, and a deafening screech started building from deep within him.

Oh Lordy please save me
Help me find my little lady
You know I'm going plum crazy
About the baby of my baby

We found the baby of my baby
Stone dead cold and blue
You know the baby of my baby
Well she was my baby too

One by one, each agent began to unravel and sob, trembling in a struggle to keep their weapons trained on their would-be captives. Buster could no longer contain himself and let loose with an ear-piercing wail that caused every agent to drop their rifles and buckle to their knees. While Red-eye had to stop playing to protect his own hearing, Buster took another swig of *Dago Red* and kept wailing to exact a bit more revenge upon the now exposed and vulnerable agents of EAR.

The plan had worked, and the guests of the Layman's Lair were safe from arrest and free to flee, which they did save for the surviving members of Beelzebunghole who were seated at the bar along the long arm of the "U" closest to the stage. The bass player, Weasel, was a chimney sweep and although Caucasian in race, was covered in splotches of dark gray and flat black. He stood up from his barstool still holding his ears. "Keep crying Buster, this show ain't over yet." The drummer, Shitropes, had white guy dreadlocks and a receding hairline. He stood up as well and nudged the singer. Lefty, who looked like a 12-year-old serial killer, stood up and mouthed the words to his band mates, "Let's fucking do this."

In the throes of misery-fueled rage, each man picked up an AR-15 dropped by a struggling EAR agent. Red-eye reacted quickly and put down the guitar, jumped off the stage, grabbed Buster by the arm and yanked him towards the door. As they breached the threshold and bounded out onto Colfax Avenue, a barrage of gunfire erupted as what was left of Beelzebunghole mowed down every EAR agent in the bar in cold blood, point blank.

Red-eye Robinson urged the Whine-o to keep up alongside him. Buster was still sniffling from the whole affair and blatantly carrying his box of wine in one hand and a cracked plastic cup in the other. They shuffled down the longest avenue in America listening to the gunfire behind them and trying to look inconspicuous.

The situation reminded Red-eye of something Pablo said to him back in the early 1980s as the punk wave washed over pop culture for the second time. Or was it the third?

"In the heart of every true punk rocker lurks profound contempt for authority. A deep-seeded festering boil of re-sentment that was long ago planted by a shitbag of some sort — an abusive parent, a violating priest, a corrupt cop, a loathsome educator, a bully, a rapist, a murderer. Given the chance to exact revenge on the figureheads of a world to which they don't relate, some punks take the high road and walk away. Those end up conceding to the stereotypes and joining society. Those are called 'poseurs.' Others resist and stay 'punk rock' for life. Those ones are regarded as just plain dangerous."

Payback's a bitch.

Chapter 38

Let's Make a Deal

Earl and Cricket hunkered down in the dim light of his apartment. As they waited for the GPS receiver to light up, each sipped on their chosen catalysts. Earl was getting better at conversation, and he found talking to Cricket particularly easy. "I never asked because I figured you'd tell me if you wanted me to know. But just for the sake of shooting the shit, where did you live before you started staying here?"

"Oh, you know … here and there. I'd crash with Pablo sometimes, but his old lady was kind of a bitch. She once told me that if I tried to take her man from her, she'd poke my eyes out and slit my throat. I stayed with friends and acquaintances, mostly guys who wanted something more until they'd finally discover my problem. Those were short-lived relationships if you even want to call them that. All that time, bouncing around from place to place, I learned something. There's a big difference between being lonely and being alone. You can feel both in a crowded room, or all by yourself you can feel neither."

170

"I know what you mean. I've always felt isolated with no one to talk to, so at some point I just gave up the idea of even trying. In a noisy bar, at work, at home, on the street — I was lonely all the time until I discovered beer and then eventually Pablo discovered me ... and then I met you."

"You lucked out there, sucker." Cricket interjected some affectionate levity and Earl began to blush. "Don't get me wrong" she continued "Being independent is really important to me. But, when you feel abandoned and it seems like there's no one who gives a shit about you, that it wouldn't matter a lick if you hung yourself, shit your pants or jumped for joy ... that's when life really sucks."

Earl expressed his agreement in the best way he knew. "Bluuuuuuuuup."

"Aside from Pablo, you're the first nice guy I've ever hung out with. I guess I had a bad habit of attracting losers and fuckups. Things are so much different now. The fact that you can be close to me and that my BANE doesn't drive you away means everything to me. I want to make sure I keep sight of how unique and unlikely our situation is and never take it for granted."

Earl saw an opportune moment and decided it would not pass him by. "I want to be with you. Always. So that you don't feel alone even if I'm not around. And when I'm here — I want to make sure our time together counts."

Cricket's eyes seemed to twinkle for a moment in the half-light. "Then do it" she winked. "If these EAR fuckers get their way, they're gonna close in and try to lock us up. I'd rather bite the big one or die fighting — knowing that I got someone worth fighting for.

"I won't ever let these motherfuckers catch us. They'll have to kill me to stop me. You have my word."

Cricket smiled with thinly veiled glee. "That's my man."

The GPS receiver lit up in Cricket's hand. They were at 6th and Pennsylvania, just north of Broadway. As the EAR vans sped south towards The Joker, they would inevitably encounter traffic congestion from throngs of Friday night Denver idiots — giving Cricket and Earl ample time to each jump onto the back of a van, climb up to the roof and ambush the agents as they piled out.

Earl was getting juiced up and felt ready. He was going to pummel them with brute belching force while Cricket's plan was blind them into submission with sear-spit, and if necessary, take them out one by one with her newly-acquired AR-15. Earl chimed in "Where are they? We'd better get going."

"My receiver says they're at Bannock and 11th heading towards Speer. Dumb fucks don't even know it's faster to take Broadway straight south than to get hemmed up in the Denver General Hospital complex."

"Either way, they're coming. We'll catch them at 6th Avenue, Let's go."

Earl grabbed his backpack bulging with cans of *Quasimodo Gold*. He paused for a moment, removed one and stuck it back in the fridge. "Always save one for later" he mumbled. Cricket shoved a pint of *Granny Slapper* into the inside pocket of her leather jacket and shouldered her rifle. She had procured one of Pablo's old trench coats for concealing the AR-15 and she threw that on last after shoving a grenade in each pocket. Just before leaving, Earl paused, "Hey Cricket, think fast," he tossed her a 1.7-ounce plastic shooter bottle of *Granny Slapper*. "Grabbed that for you at the last liquor store run." She slipped it into the breast pocket of her leather jacket.

"Thanks, you cheap sonofabitch," she joked. "I'll hang onto it for later."

Within a minute the two were jogging west on 6th Avenue, quickly covering the few blocks between their hideout and Broadway Blvd. They stopped at the northeast corner of 6th and Broadway, trying to stroll inconspicuously along the south entrance of the Last National Bank. Earl was ready for battle. "Cricket" he whispered, "Where are these bastards?" She glanced down at the GPS receiver, shook it, wiped off the screen and looked again.

"They're stopped a few blocks to the northwest at 8th and Delaware."

"What the fuck is over there? The hospital, right?"

"Yeah."

"What the hell are they doing?"

"I don't know but our mission tonight is to stop those fuckers before they can do any more damage, and that's exactly what we're going to do."

Before going dead, the signal's last ping was at the northwest corner of the Denver General Hospital complex. They arrived in a full sprint to find just one empty EAR van parked halfway on the east sidewalk, facing south against oncoming traffic.

Earl looked up at the letter on the building. "What the fuck is Pavilion C?"

"Oh, holy sweet motherfucking Jesus."

"What?"

Cricket swallowed hard. "This is the maternity ward." She involuntarily placed her right hand on her abdomen, recalling the unnerving news rendered by their last visit to Parental Planninghood.

Earl cracked a beer and began chugging. Cricket grabbed his shoulder, but not hard enough to make him stop drinking. "Don't start wrecking agents until we get them out of the building. We can't just waltz in behind them ..."

Earl was done chugging a moment later and belched "BACK DOOR." Cricket took a swig of tequila, and deftly rotated the rifle strap up from under her left arm, getting her right hand on the grip and her other on the barrel. They sprinted up Delaware to 8th, took a right and another into the gangway between the C and B buildings. Cricket scanned the scene, "There it is — the service entrance." They shuffled up to the door and Earl inhaled, swallowed some air and clenched his fists in preparation to blow it off the hinges. "Hold on hot head" Cricket whispered. "Call me crazy but don't you think we out to at least *try* and be stealthy for a minute?"

"Good point." Earl exhaled and puffed his cheeks a few times like he was trying not to puke. "Well," he gulped "Can you at least loosen up the lock for me?" Cricket took another swig of *Granny Slapper*, swished it around and spurt a thin arc between the door and the doorjamb. The saliva hissed as it began to corrode the metal lock assembly. Earl focused his intent on producing a quick, dense blast. "Hit it again," he urged. She spat into the crack again. Earl waited a few seconds and shoved out a belch that sounded like grunt from a silverback gorilla. The burst broke the bolt from the door frame slot without a massive racket.

"Nice one, champ."

"Could have been louder, that's for sure."

"Don't matter. They're up a few floors by now anyways. Chug another one, we've got five flights of stairs to climb."

By the fourth floor landing Earl and Cricket could hear the screaming. Halfway up the fifth flight, the familiar stench of methane was seeping beneath the stairwell exit door. The Belcher chugged another beer, Cricket clicked the safety button to the "off" position on her AR-15. "Goddammit," she spat. "It's that smelly-assed creep again. I thought we left him for dead under that collapsed rooftop. Fuck me running ... now what?"

Earl had a plan. "As soon as you shove open the door, I'll blast a belch through there to clear the fumes so we can breathe." She twisted the handle and pushed, the Belcher stepped across the threshold and huffed out a swift gust of gut gas that made the thick haze dissipate.

The fifth floor of Pavilion C was a busy place for a Friday night. Nurses, orderlies, OBGYNs and patients were scattered about the floor — each sprawled out in an impromptu snooze position caused by noxious vapors from the Gasser's freshly-healed anus. Among the unconscious were misplaced personnel from a nearby facility of a far different purpose — the Dinnermen. The 12 agents were bumbling about on the floor, tweaking on MORE and transfixed in an enhanced buzz like a bunch of freshly injected junkies who just passed around the nitrous tank.

Cricket trained her rifle from one side of the room to the other while Earl reached for another beer. "Where is that motherfucker!?" she demanded.

In a patient room halfway down the hall from the stairwell

175

entrance, the shrieks continued. Having cornered his prey at last, the Gasser was living out his long-lusted fantasy. He had, alas, availed himself to a woman going into labor. Minutes before Earl and Cricket arrived, he had partially sedated her with a mild gassing, slathered his right hand with sanitizer and drove it up her birth canal like he was throwing an uppercut. The mother awoke screaming and wailing in mortal agony as Luther Fisk finally pulled forth the ultimate bludgeon — an innocent life – and used it to dispatch his eternal enemy — a creator of life. He swung the fetus by its neck and banged it against its mother's face a she screamed in horror and bled out.

He emerged from the patient room chewing on the dead baby's left cheek and saw Earl and Cricket at the end of the corridor. He hucked the tiny carcass of blood and afterbirth down the hall like crimson bowling ball which slid past Earl and Cricket and came to a stop amid the cluster of Dinnermen, who descended upon it like vultures on fresh roadkill. The Gasser used the diversion to duck into the adjacent nursery to commandeer a bit of leverage.

"Well, well, well …" his voice was like the rusty hinges on an outhouse door. "It's my two favorite lovebirds, come to sing to me again." He stepped out of the nursery holding a small bundle in the crook of his left arm while positioning his respirator atop his head with his right. "I'd have you hum me a little lullaby for this sweet little baby, but she's already asleep."

The Dinnermen were all wiping their mouths and standing up again, unlike the rest of the comatose inhabitants of the maternity ward. The elite squad had been given explicit orders from Blatherskite to follow the Gasser's every command. Their chemically-dependent brain cells had just tasted a new kind of high on top of the everyday MORE buzz. And now, each was looking at his new dealer with the growing adoration of a dope addict who had just discovered speedballs. They had discovered that inhaling the flatulence of a MORE addict can heighten a MORE buzz already in progress.

Earl could feel his blood beginning to boil, "I'm warning you right now, you sick fuck. You put that child back where it belongs or I'll —"

"You'll what," the Gasser cut him off. "Burp the baby to death?"

The Dinnermen began laughing, applauding, whistling and slapping each other on the back.

"Comport yourselves you fools and stand at the ready!" The Gasser scolded his new comrades with bitter affection as he placed his gaze on Cricket. "Easy now, lava lips, or my silly gang of homicidal twitch cases are going to assist me in killing every innocent child, pathetic mother and sappy worker in this entire ward. Your firepower and your bellicose boyfriend might be able to stop me, but not without dipping your mitts elbow deep into a river of brat blood."

Earl was counting the EAR agents and calculating the distance, trajectory and spread it would take to slam them all sideways with one belch blast. Cricket lowered her rifle. "What do you want?"

The Gasser smiled with delight. "Moi? Well … you see this little bundle of joy here? I want to march down the hallway to her sleeping mother's room and beat the bitch to death with her own worthless progeny. Now that I've finally accomplished my beautiful dream, I intend to do it again and again."

Earl interjected, "C'mon man, hand over the kid. We'll put down the beers and guns and you can just leave without getting maimed, shot or arrested. Deal?"

"I'll tell you what. I'll swap you for it." Earl and Cricket looked askance at one another and the Gasser continued, "my benefactor wants to get his hands on poison puss over here and eventually on her dope smoking amigo — Pablo Vasquez. I have been commissioned to act as negotiator and courier."

"No fucking way, man." Earl was ready to offer himself up instead.

"Tough shit, Perry Mason. This little diaper pirate is my bargaining chip and you are running out of time. The hospital staff are beginning to stir. If I am forced to break wind again to put them back down and give you the fight you thirst for, I can guarantee this sweet little newborn baby will die a very violent, tragic, neck-breaking death — and it will be all your fault."

Cricket slowly knelt and placed her rifle on the floor. "OK asshole. Give the child to Earl."

"C'mon, Cricket, no … let's take these fuckers out!" He pleaded.

"No baby. You'll find a way, I trust you. I can't let him do this again. We can't risk him killing another kid." She looked at the Gasser and then to the EAR squadron. "Watch it, shitheads. He's got a gullet full of beer, and he'll take your fucking heads off if you try anything stupid."

The Dinnermen's squad leader pointed his pistol at Cricket. "Hands on your head, walk this way slowly."

"Fuck that," barked Earl. "The kid first." The Dinnermen slowly moved in as the Gasser approached the Belcher. The poisoned child was beginning to stir, struggling to breathe properly in order to muster a scream that would rival that of the Whine-o. The Belcher set his beer down on the nurse station counter and reached out to take the bundle of new life from the clutches of putrid, reeking evil. He looked into the Gasser's bloodshot green eyes. "I'm going to take your goddamn head off, you filthy bastard."

"Tsk, tsk, tsk," Luther clicked. "Don't swear in front of the child, please."

The Dinnermen led Cricket away in the midst of a marching formation with the Gasser at the rear. He stopped and whisked around, "Oh yeah — nice try with the GPS trackers, by the way. I took the other one off the second EAR van before I sent it over to decimate The Joker. Looks like you blew it twofold tonight, Mr. Belcher. If I were you, I'd say 'excuse me.'"

"Don't listen to him," Cricket called over her shoulder as the group stepped into the elevator. Earl could hear fear in her voice for the first time. "And Earl," she shouted "don't you leave me alone with these assholes for too long, you hear me? Don't leave me alo —"

The elevator closed on her shout. Earl stood there in shock, holding a newborn baby in the middle of a murder-scene-maternity ward. The security cameras, if the Gasser didn't disable them, would tell the tale of what transpired but still — his current position did not paint him in a good light. He waited for the woman behind the nurse station counter to rise to her feet and regain her awareness. He then handed her the crying child, picked up Cricket's rifle and disappeared back down the stairwell.

Chapter 39

Hang Time

The basement level of EAR Headquarters reeked like an unventilated slaughterhouse on a hot day. The EAR van carrying The Gasser, the Dinnermen and Cricket pulled in through the automated doors Earl and Cricket had infiltrated two nights prior. Cricket was led through the double doors at the end of the rectangular parking enclosure. After the devouring of Luna, the elite squad and the unlikely collaborator in their midst had developed a taste for human flesh that was expanding in tandem with their addiction to MORE. Cricket gagged after three steps into the mess area, "Good lord have you slobs ever heard of mopping before? It smells like a herd of hobos died of dysentery in here."

The Gasser was quick to retort, "Well, that's not exactly the case — but close enough." He giggled at his ambiguous hinting and then continued, "They were definitely bumming, that's for damn sure. Instead of lobotomizing would-be dissenters, my benefactor has taken to reappropriating their latent calories to fuel his elite division. The Dinnermen always get the deserters."

"Do me a favor, stinky," Cricket was determined to keep her game face intact. "Will you at least take these damn cuffs off me? I'm not a threat to you and your gang of butt buddies."

"Not a chance, pussypants. Not until we talk about the elusive Pablo Vasquez and how he needs to come have a little chat with his old friend Blatherskite." As he leered at Cricket, two of the Dinnermen rifled through her trench coat — removing the grenades and extra clips of 223-gauge bullets for the AR-15. "String her up in one of the holding cells and then go tell your boss I've delivered his order." The Dinnermen obediently scurried off, eager to do the Gasser's bidding.

Upstairs in the penthouse suite, Blatherskite twitched with delight at the exchange as he watched from the CCTV monitors. The MORE was piled up on his desk like a mini Mt. Fuji and the mirror on the dope tray revealed that his consumption was taking a visual toll. The compounds in his nose candy were killing the circulation in the outer tissues of his facial skin, causing outer layers to cease regeneration and regress towards his skull. The result was a gaunt complexion marred by gaping nostrils, widened eye sockets and cracked, receding lips.

Meanwhile the molecular spectrum of Luther Fisk's intestinal vapors had pushed the threshold of his olfactory perception. Instead of deadening the nerves in his nose, his own stench had pushed them to the edge of their capacity which caused them to adapt and become stronger. As he foraged for a snack in the basement mess, he wondered about Cricket's distinct scent. He pondered the aroma while nibbling at the rib of a recently-recruited gamer turned cannibalized dissenter. "Alas," he sang, "Now that tastes like a sugar-fed calf suckled in a fenced-off lazy boy." He pensively tapped a bloody rib bone against his forehead. "What are you hiding from me, my little bug?" He wondered aloud.

Cricket's arms were restrained above her head with the chain of the handcuffs run between a sewer pipe and the ceiling and her clamped wrists swelling on either side. Although the upper portions of the EAR building were relatively new, they were built upon a pre-existing foundation that was once annexed by the Denver Police Department. This wing of the basement was all holding cells. It was neglected and, in some areas, downright dilapidated. The air was stale with the musty old-building smell of crumbling brick, cracked concrete, peeling paint and fraying asbestos. The walls looked like tepid swamp water on an overcast day and glowed sickly in the pallid fluorescent light. The Gasser darkened the doorway of Cricket's cell. "Did my methed-up fart snarfers miss something?" He toyed.

"Yeah," Cricket spat back. "Your ugly face the last time they decided to rip one apart and eat it."

"Is everything that comes out of your mouth so exquisitely nasty?"

"Come closer and find out. I dare you."

The Gasser stepped toward her within a couple feet, slipped his hand to the inside lapel of her leather jacket, pulled out her pint of *Granny Slapper* and flinched backwards just in time for a wad of spit to barely miss his face. "Lemme guess," he giggled. "That little spate of hatred would have been quite a bit more lethal with a little of this?"

"Talk all the shit you want, assface. Pablo and Earl are going come in here, mow you down and drain the shit from between your ears one kick at a time."

"Ah, yes, Pablo — we'll get to him in a minute, but right now I want to see this stuff be put to its higher purpose. I want to see your stinging spit turn lethal, but you can't just have a swig or two. You gotta chug the whole thing."

Cricket hesitated where she normally wouldn't. "Yeah, sure. No problem." She looked down.

"Hmmmmm." He was prodding at her like a cat nudging at a half-dead mouse. "I don't believe you. Why the hesitancy?"

"I'm … I'm actually trying to cut back."

"Oh really? Since when do boozeheads go to Parental Planninghood when they're 'trying to cut back?'" He un-screwed the lid, took a slug and smashed the bottle against the back wall as Cricket's means of escape trickled onto the floor.

"Ah hah! Yes! Alas!" He began to dance in a circle. "This is the ultimate treasure — my very own pregnant woman to do with whatever I choose. Once again, I can exact my revenge for being born, this time in an opus of deliberate pageantry. Hallelujah! I am going to tuck you away tight and fatten you up nicely. Then, when you're plump as a ripe plum, I am going to host the party of the year with you and your progeny as the honored guests of evening fare."

Cricket's face scrunched into a glaring scowl of determination. "I should have stuck my boot up your ass when I had the chance."

"Shoulda, woulda, coulda," He taunted as he bent over, clenched his fists and discharged a deluge of gag vapor that caused Cricket to choke, gasp for air and then pass out limp, hanging from both bleeding wrists.

"That's right. Nap it up, ya little mother."

The Gasser slammed the cell door shut behind him. As he walked down the musty corridor towards the kitchen, he was followed by several of the Dinnermen — slinking after him like dogs behind a master who has two pockets full of bacon. "Where the fuck is Blatherskite!? I want to renegotiate!"

A few minutes later, Cricket stirred. The Gasser's fumes had caused her eyes to water and, head hung low, she saw two trails of singed leather running down her jacket on either side of the zipper seam. In the mess hall at the end of the basement corridor she could hear the Gasser's growl being challenged by another voice jabbering at rapid-fire speed.

"She's mine. I found her and I'm going to keep her." Luther was bracing for a fight to the death.

"God dammit you stinking sack of skunk piss. The only reason she is here is to lure in Vasquez. Until I have him, nothing is being renegotiated. Do you hear me, you tuna boat shithouse?"

"OK fine, Skeletor, but you don't have to get personal about it. Gimme a phone and I'll make sure she gets him down here. No sweat."

"Dinnermen Squad Leader! Bring me the remote phone unit. The landline receiver is in the closet next to the walk-in. And for the rest of you cunts, clean this fucking place up!"

Back in Cricket's cell, Blatherskite and the Gasser stood at a respectful distance as one of the Dinnermen held the cordless phone to Cricket's face. On the other end was the incessant ring of Pablo's landline. He picked it up without saying 'hello' and instead, just listened. "Pablo, goddammit I know you're there. Look, man. These assholes are trying to get me to get you to walk into a death trap. Forget it. I can handle these cunts myse —" Blatherskite slapped Cricket's face away and snatched the phone from the Dinnerman.

"Hello, my dear ol' pal. I am simply requesting that you accept my cordial invitation to pay me a visit. Otherwise, I am going to impose upon this little friend of yours the same terrible punishment I exacted on Luna when she came here to sell you out. She was delicious, by the way."

"OK, shitmouth. I'm on the way."

Chapter 40

Prelude to Battle

Earl concealed Cricket's AR-15 within his backpack as best he could — the barrel protruding conspicuously from the top. Luckily, every cop in downtown Denver was busy cleaning up and processing the night's quadruple scenes of city-wide chaos.

When Knockers opened the door to Pablo's place, the look on Earl's face put her, Pablo, Red-eye and the Whine-o on edge. "Where's Cricket?" she asked.

Earl was on the border of hysteria, pacing about and trying to relate what just happened. "They found the GPS trackers and lured us away. Cricket gave herself up to stop the Gasser and his men from killing another baby. They must have taken her to EAR Headquarters. I came back for supplies, but I'm going back over there right goddamn now an I swear I'm going to kill every last one of those mother —"

"Hang on, kid." Pablo interrupted. "You need to calm down for just a minute and get your head together."

"I … I know … I may be a little drunk, but I remember what the Gasser said" Just then the phone rang and everyone in Pablo's apartment froze. After a few rings he walked over to the receiver perched on the wall between bookshelves, picked it up and listened. After a long minute, he muttered something and hung up.

The Soothsayer turned and began, "The time has come for me to put a stop to EAR by decapitating snake at the head of the helm. But the truth is, I can't do it without you — all of you. Look at it this way, with martial law on the horizon and every means of escaping the city blocked off, it's just a matter of days before time runs out for all of us. We each have a better chance at survival — of outrunning the running out of time — if we stick together and move on EAR and the National Guard as a team. It's better to die out there fighting than to live in here hiding. Besides, Cricket is one of us, and right now she's in there gagging on the Gasser's butt bombs and enduring an endless harangue from the world's biggest windbag … both of whom will eventually kill her."

Earl was beginning to calm down enough for conversation. "OK asshole, I'm all ears."

Knockers, Red-eye and the Whine-o leaned in, equally curious as to what was percolating in Pablo's head.

"First, you three boozeheads need to hydrate, sleep, sober up, eat and hydrate again. I am devising specific ways for each of you to bolster your BANE. Knockers, get some R and R as well — and thanks — ours was the only team tonight whose mission didn't end in a bloodshed clusterfuck."

Red-eye relished some good ol' mean-spirited banter. "Fuck you, blubbermug. Are you sure you don't want to wail out one last sniffle tune while you still have time?"

"If we somehow get through this, I'll sob like a sissy all night to your heart's content."

"Chickenshit," spat Knockers.

"Crybaby," sneered the Whine-o.

"OK then, be back in 12 hours and don't do anything stupid that'll get you caught. I have to go commandeer more supplies. After tomorrow night, this town will never be the same."

15 minutes later, Earl trudged into his apartment, half expecting Cricket to be there. He was heartbroken, lovesick and gagging on emotional gore. He opened his refrigerator and looked at the lone can of *Quasimodo Gold* he'd left hours before. "I swear to you Cricket, I'm going to get you out one way or another. I won't leave you alone."

Meanwhile, down in the stench of the EAR basement, Cricket hung by her wrists while Blatherskite expounded his systemic disgust for The Soothsayer in a jabbering tirade. He paced back and forth in the cell flapping his arms and yelling as though Pablo was strung up before him "Ridicule me once, twice, thrice not very fucking nice – ungrateful traitor. You think you're so goddamn funny, so exquisitely clever with your little smoke-and-mirror parlor tricks. You think you're hot shit — taking insurmountable risks just to try and ruin my life and make a mockery of me? Well who's the pissant now, huh, Mr. Pablo Vasquez? See what I've become because of your stupid little hardy-har pranks? I'm going to cherish every moment of your suffering you self-righteous washed up flimflamming fuckwad."

The Gasser stood by, snacking on rubbery half-rotten celery stalks like they were ropes of licorice and trying to stave off his mounting addiction to MORE. "That's right,

Blatherskite — keep haranguing this little twat cuz she's got his number. Look at her, she's probably got his dick tied around her little finger. She'll bring him here, and he'll be forced to surrender or watch her die."

Blatherskite continued his diatribe, trailing off as he wandered down the corridor headed to get some MORE.

Cricket wisely kept her opinion to herself, but couldn't help mutter quietly, "Jesus, dude. Get over yourself, will ya?"

The next morning, as the fog of Earl's hangover began to recede, the full gravity of the situation began to settle onto his shoulders. With clarity of mind came a trembling notion of electric rage. For once, his purpose in life was clearly laid out before him — unmistakable, blatant and pure. His was going to decimate everyone and everything between him and Cricket.

On his way over to Pablo's place, he peered around from beneath his hoodie. The streets were mostly deserted, populated only by National Guard Infantry trucks and Humvees heading west towards the State Capitol and Civic Center Park. When he trudged back into the hideout, the rest of the gang was already there.

Red-eye was whipping up a breakfast of bacon, eggs and toast while the Whine-o was removing a bag of *Dago Red* from within its box. Knockers' back was to the door as she faced Pablo and he seemed to be affixing some sort of harness to her torso. The assembly had a thick powerlifting belt-like supporting back arch leading upward to two back-pack-like shoulder straps. Pablo's head popped up from in front of her right shoulder to greet him. "Ah, yes! Just in time amigo! Earl, I'd like to introduce you to a new way of viewing.

Knockers rotated to reveal a contraption with four frontal stabilizers — two protruding from the waist and one from each shoulder — all meeting at a centralized camera-mounting frame. Only, instead of a camera, Pablo had affixed the biggest magnifying glass Earl had ever seen, positioned directly in front of Knockers' bosom. She could barely contain her glee "Goddammit, Pablo! You're a modern day Leonardo motherfuckin' DaVinci!" It was clear that as soon as she exposed her chest, the hypnotic power of her bust would be amplified by the beveled glass — bolstering her BANE with maximum impact and giving her the drop on anyone who faced her.

Red-eye Robinson shoved a forkful of scrambled eggs into his mouth and spoke while he chewed. "Sit down and eat, Earl."

Pablo was securing the Velcro straps of Knockers' harness. There was a twinge of trepidation in his voice as he cautioned her, "Be careful where you point that thing, mamacita, it's untested so there's no telling how devastating you're going to be."

"You wanna find out again, daddy-o?"

"Ha ha. Jesus, man — I treat you right, help you out, and you chew it up and spit it back at me. Typical bitch."

"That's right, asshole. OK fine. Thanks, I guess."

The sarcasm and harsh banter did little to diminish Earl's emotional state. Pablo quietly moved on to his next set of BANE-boasting contraptions — a series of three identical assemblies comprised of an amplified speaker mounted to a heavy-duty body harness made for chest-mount cameras, reengineered for audio. Instead of digital visual technology, each harness was equipped with a Warbler Cicada brand powered amplifier and a head-mounted microphone/ear bud set plugged into the clean channel. "Red-eye, Whine-o — these babies will allow us to project our voices hands-free so that we can extend our BANE to targets that would normally be out of range.

"Hot damn!" blurted Red-eye — scrambled eggs falling from his mouth.

"How much does that ugly-ass thing weigh?" worried the Whine-o as he nibbled on a piece of toast.

"Don't fuss, you little crybaby." Pablo was abrasively reassuring. "These suckers only weigh about five pounds. Just don't spill any *Dago Red* on the electronics and you'll be fine."

Pablo stepped over to his guitars and picked up the Nickel-plated Resonator Ukulele. He cradled it, mashed the strings down hard and strummed a few bars. "Hey, Red-eye," he called over his shoulder.

"What? I'm eating, dammit."

"I want you to take this with you. Just in case the spirit moves you, if you know what I mean."

"Jesus, man. Are we going to war or going to play a gig?"

"It's the same thing for some. Just agree that you'll take it, OK?"

"Righto, daddy-o."

Meanwhile, Earl was sick with worry but was forcing himself to eat. "I don't mean to be self-centered," he mumbled through a mouthful of breakfast, "but all this gear begs the question. Do you have some sort of a BANE booster for me?"

Pablo didn't look up from the harness straps he was adjusting on Buster and answered matter-of-factly "No kid, you've got all the boost you'll ever need. You're special. You know why? You're in love." The words hung in the air between the five of them as Earl gulped down a half-chewed lump of bacon and blinked like a dog watching television. Red-eye and the Whine-o burst into laughter followed by the hearty howl of Knockers and the squinting chuckle of the Soothsayer. "Sorry, kid. I couldn't help myself."

Earl almost managed a grin but was again overcome by the urge to slug Pablo right in the teeth. "Ah-ha!" Pablo ribbed. "There it is, amigo. That rage you've got buried deep down in your guts. You've got to bring it to a surface boil and keep it there — otherwise you can forget this mission completely."

"Yep. I know." Earl pivoted his anger to the plate in front of him and devoured with a grudge.

"Speaking of harnessing," Pablo re-established the tactical tone of the mission prep. "I've got a special surprise for you. Ever hear of Cornelius?"

"Biblical guy, right?"

"Yeah, something like that. A bit of a turncoat, but that don't matter. Check this out …" Pablo pointed to two 23-inch tall cylinders parked between two of his guitars. "These, my friend, are Cornelius kegs of *Quasimodo Gold* — the last two in stock at Astronaut Liquors. Do you remember that scuba diving harness we snagged on the Castle Sports raid?"

"Yeah."

"Well, instead of two compressed air tanks in the harness slots, you'll carry kegs — each with a tapped nozzle at the ready."

"Holy shit," Earl was awestruck. "I am going to kick the living fuck out those assholes!"

Knockers chimed in, "None so righteous as the newly converted."

"Look kid," Pablo continued, "We're basing our guerilla assault on EAR around your destructive abilities. We are your support, but the fact of the matter is that you are the main source of firepower. Knockers is going to set them up, and you're going to knock 'em down."

Pablo walked over to the kegs and admired his ingenuity with a grin.

"No pressure eh?" Earl muttered.

"Oh, they're pressurized for sure." Pablo crouched down and knocked on each keg twice.

The five comrades sat at Pablo's table and hashed out the details of their mission to sandbag the National Guard, to cripple EAR and to extract Cricket from the clutches of Blatherskite. Pablo pulled a large blueprint from a cylindrical container and rolled it out in front of Red-eye and the Whine-o, each seated on either side of him. Earl thought he recognized the white cardboard tube. "Hey, where did you get that?"

"What, this? At your old grind. Security at the Denver Public Library has always been lax. I think those people smoke too much dope." Pablo gazed proudly over the blueprints which were schematics for a series of underground tunnels that connected every building adjacent to Denver's Civic Center Park including the State Capitol, the City and County Building, the Denver County Courthouse and EAR Headquarters as well as several ancillary businesses on Capitol Hill.

"Red-eye," Pablo began "According to this, there's an entry point into these tunnels a few blocks northeast of EAR HQ in the basement of The Senate Lounge. You and Buster can gain access there and make your way southwest. There's a GPS locator still intact under one of the EAR vans, use your transmitter to find an opportune entry point into the basement level of EAR. I'll meet you two on the inside."

Red-eye rubbed his chin and mused "I've heard of these so-called tunnels, but I reckoned they were just an urban legend. Old-school Denver folks sometimes say, during Prohibition, government officials used them to smuggle booze and whores into the Capitol Building."

"Bullshit." Buster interjected. "They'd use the tunnels to sneak away while they were supposed to be working to chug booze and bang prostitutes."

Knockers chimed in, "Same damn thing, assholes."

"All right magpies. Don't everyone blow their wad yapping it up before the big soiree."

"Lemme guess," Earl began. "Knockers and I are going to take out a couple squadrons on Colfax near the State Capitol to create a diversion so you can access EAR without getting your head blown off, right?"

"Bingo, kid." Pablo didn't miss a beat. "That's why you've got the big guns. There's more artillery in those kegs than bullets in a well-armed platoon. They know we're holed up somewhere in Capitol Hill, so they've anticipated an onslaught from the east — that's why we must split up and move in from different directions."

"Lay it on us, Padrino." Knockers was emboldened by her new accessory.

Pablo split his index and middle fingers into a "V" shape and pointed at Earl and Knockers. "You two are going to create an initial diversion at the detainee holding station at Colfax and Washington by infiltrating the area from the north. Wait until 10:00 PM to strike. I'll be making my way into EAR from the south ..." He dropped his hand and scanned across the eyes of his four friends and continued, "This is war and they are here to eradicate us, and anyone like us. They will kill you on sight without question, so fight like your life depends on it — because it does."

15 blocks to the west, the EAR HQ building was a wasp nest of activity. The recent declaration of martial law had made Blatherskite, the Gasser, the Dinnermen and even the lowest grunts in the mouth-breathing ranks of EAR excited by the power of unmerited authority. Blatherskite insisted on supervising the concocting, packaging and distribution of the latest potency of MORE. At all hours, he would stomp about the shop floor shouting arbitrary commands laced with the promise of extended MORE-induced euphoria for all who complied.

"Goddammit you Dinnermen! Get me another kilo of meth in here you fucking retards! I swear on the bleeding eyeballs of the mother of Jesus H. fucking Christ I want this next batch of MORE to raise the goddamn dead! Do you motherfuckers hear me?"

Having witnessed Earl's power firsthand, The Gasser was sure that The Belcher would come calling for Cricket and he planned accordingly. He skittered about in a hand-wringing frenzy — attempting to engineer his exoneration by imagining the role he would play in a full-scale battle. He imagined that his heroic flatulence would earn him unlimited access to his prey and her progeny. He was reeling at the idea of continuing to live out his fantasies without recourse. Foraging through the stores of EAR rations, he had amassed a fart-spawning fricassee of delights including EAR cadet cadaver scraps, cream of broccoli soup and pickled artichoke hearts.

Just down the corridor from the mess hall, Cricket could hear The Gasser snarfing down mouthfuls of methane-producing slop. She pulled herself upwards, swung her pelvis towards the large PVC pipe she was handcuffed to, then rotated her right hip upwards and counterclockwise while pulling her left hand downward. Once atop the pipe, sandwiched between it and the ceiling, she began working the plastic shooter bottle of *Granny Slapper* from her left breast pocket by pushing her left shoulder into the pipe. Knowing damn well that melting the plastic meant she would untether herself in a deluge of EAR agent feces, she wrapped her right arm around the underside of the pipe and up the left side so that her left hand could pull the bottle free.

Meanwhile, Red-eye Robinson and the Whine-o made their way down 13th Avenue against what would have been oncoming traffic had the streets not been deserted. The Whine-o laid it on Red-eye. "Man, I've never seen Capitol Hill so empty before. Gives me the creeps."

"Look Buster, once we get inside the Senate Lounge, you can moan and groan to your sniffle heart's content. But for now, we need to stay in the shadows and shut the fuck up." The curfew set by martial law forced the Senate Lounge to close early for the first time in 40 years. After prying the back door open, they went behind the bar and found the hatch to the basement. "You think you had the creeps out there, do ya?" Red-eye's tone was grave. "Just wait until we descend."

"I don't like this, Red-eye." As they crept down, Red-eye noticed d a bottle of *Badger's Breath* on the bar shelf. "I always loved this place," he mumbled.

The hatch to the Prohibition tunnels was hidden beneath years of booze boxes and musty bar towels. The hinges squeaked like rusty hardware on an old barn door and the corridor exhaled a gasp of dusty air that hadn't been hacked on in over half a century. Buster began to whimper. "Here's to hoping these flashlight batteries we lifted are juiced up good or this is gonna really suck. Goddammit, Red-eye. I'm scared of the dark." He took a slug of wine to settle his nerves. They crouched next to the tunnel entrance as Red-eye spread the blueprint schematics across the basement floor. Their path would lead them west, parallel to Colfax Avenue and then south between Grant and Lincoln streets. They would pass directly beneath the State Capitol, hang another right at 14th Street and head west again through the final stretch of tunnel that would place them directly beneath the EAR HQ building at 14th and Bannock streets. Buster hung his head down into the hole and pointed his flashlight into the void. Although their trek was a mere four blocks, the ominous, brick-laden path below them seemed more like a journey of 1,000 miles.

Red-eye prepared to descend while Buster fidgeted with his harness. "Hang on, please" he whined. "I need another slug of lobotomy sauce to deal with this fucking bullshit."

"Yep," agreed Red-eye. "I don't like to drink before showtime but tonight I'm gonna make an exception." He took a pull at his bottle of *Badger's Breath*, lit a road flare and dropped it in the hole."

Buster thought he saw something move down below. "What the fuck was that?"

"Really?" Red-eye was incredulous. "We're dropping into an underground corridor that was abandoned 70-some-odd years ago and you think the rats haven't taken the damn thing over? That *Dago Red* really is making you stupid."

"Oh, shut up you wanna-be smooth-ass cool cat. You're just as freaked out as I am."

"I hear rats love wine, so you'd better not trip and fall."

Lack of moisture within the tunnel had kept the ancient wooden ladder left behind by bootleggers intact and Red-eye descended first. By the time Buster was standing next to him, the whining began. Their flashlights darted about as they assimilated the environment. The ancient tunnel was like a cross between a catacombs and an old mining shaft. "C'mon, Whine-o." Red-eye began cautiously walking. "Cricket is in trouble and we need to stop fucking around."

On the streets above the two men, Pablo Vasquez traversed Capitol Hill, passing amid the fortified centers of local and state government like a ghost. The golden-domed State Capitol building that had long towered over the squalor-ridden district of Capitol Hill somehow seemed vulnerable with military trucks parked at every intersection. Civic Center Park, the taxpayer-funded spectacle that served as an open-air flophouse and drug market — stretched across the entirety of three city blocks between the Capitol Building and the Denver County Courthouse. The usually teeming complex of grass pitches, fountains, statues and pathways was deserted save for pigeons, squirrels and the ever-present adornments of fast food wrappers, discarded clothing and anonymous piles of bum dung.

Across Colfax Avenue and two blocks east of the gilded dome of governance — the twin spires of the Cathedral Basilica of the Immaculate Conception rose like a great concrete hand making the "rock on" devil horns — perhaps in mockery of the fallacy of the separation of church and state. Fitting, that the longest and arguably seediest stretch of asphalt in North America serve as a symbolic division of two institutions that are inexorably linked. As the recently-imported spotlights darted across Capitol Hill looking for would-be saboteurs, The Soothsayer slipped unnoticed into the Golden Triangle district, and posted up just south of EAR HQ near the Clyfford Still Museum to intercept Blatherskite's meth supplier.

Chapter 41

The War on Drugs

The Belcher and Knockers circumvented the artillery trap that was set for them on Capitol Hill. They headed east from Pablo's place 10 blocks to York Street and then four blocks north to 17th Avenue. From there, they began ambling their way west again towards Washington Street where the Denver Police Department parking lot was being used as a massive holding pen for recent arrestees. Knockers was getting agitated with all the scrambling around in circles and began complaining to Earl in hushed tones. "Man, this contraption Pablo fit me with is awkward as fuck. I look like a fat bitch."

"I hear that. I'm humping way too much weight. I hope we get into some shit soon so I can empty these kegs."

"Oh Jesus, you lush. You've been sucking down that *Quasimodo Gold* for the last five blocks."

"All this walking is making me thirsty."

The Denver Police Department and its adjacent parking lot occupied the entire block between 16th Avenue and Colfax and Washington and Pearl streets. Two layers of

20-foot high electric fences topped with coils of razor wire surrounded a series of holding pens for men, women and children in various states of processing before being hauled off to permanent facilities. Hastily-erected guard towers equipped with floodlights and snipers stood at the north and south ends of the pen. Earl and Knockers assessed the situation from behind two trees on the north side of 16th Avenue. "How many?" Earl wondered.

"Guards or prisoners?"

"Both."

"I'd say 10 guards on the ground and two or three in each tower — some EAR, some military and some DPD. As far as the cage goes, I'm thinking anywhere between 250 and 400 prisoners.

"Damn," Earl mumbled, taking a hefty pull from the left side Cornelius keg tap. Knockers stepped from the shadows and crossed 16th Street towards the prisoner compound. As she stepped up onto the curb hands free with Glocks holstered, she whisked the trench coat lapels to either side and revealed the magnifying disc aimed straight into the crevice of her cleavage. The motion triggered the spotlights from the guard towers which lit her up immediately. Every set of unobstructed eyes stared straight into the lens — and soldiers, EAR agents, DPD officers and prisoners were suddenly stunned into a menagerie of mouth-gaping, stupefied poses. Knockers knew the timing of her cleavage shock clock to the nanosecond. "Now, Belcher!" she called. Earl took off from his perch, running at full speed towards the compound while sucking down *Quasimodo Gold*. He stopped three steps past Knockers and the gas in his guts seemed to keep moving with his momentum as a deafening "BLAAAAUUUP" flew from his mouth in a focused blast that echoed across the compound and collided with the far tower. The spotlights shattered, the wooden platform exploded into a confetti toss of splinters and the soldiers hit the ground in a bone crunching pile.

Earl launched another decimation at the near tower as Knockers pulled her pistols and held them at hip level, being sure not to obscure anyone's view of her chest. Earl took another pull of beer and Knockers yelled, "Get the fences, Earl and I'll keep them gawking!" She had long held a deep-seated contempt for government-sanctioned male authority figures, and she took exquisite delight at so many of them bound to her mercy. "Fuck it," she snarled, taking aim at the face of the nearest cop. Before she could plug him, Earl flexed out a guttural roar that bent the fence posts in their holes and ripped the chain link fencing and razor wire apart — causing it to flap about like ribbons tied to the front grate of a box fan. The blast made Knockers miss while the prisoners and guards were snapped from their stasis as they were flung towards the south end of the compound into a jumbled pile of jailers and the jailed.

Knockers quickly recognized Jake from the bookstore. He had landed atop an EAR agent who was struggling to regain his composure. "Jake," she screamed. "Grab his goddamn gun!" Earl seconded the notion, but as he tried to yell out the command a belch erupted from his gullet that carried the words away in a roaring "GRAB THEIR MOTHERFUCKING GUNS!" Jake pointed the rifle into the EAR agent's forehead and the other prisoners were emboldened as the rest of the guards were gripped by fear, as the barriers between them and their prisoners had been erased and they were grossly outnumbered. In a matter of a seconds, every EAR agent, soldier and DPD officer was disarmed by civilians and looking down the barrel of their own weapon.

Knockers relished the sight, but Earl was adamant,

"Knockers, we gotta keep moving. They can follow us if they want, but we must continue the assault."

They turned and headed south, and as they approached Colfax, a barrage of gunfire erupted followed by screams of agony and cheers of triumph.

"Guess the treatment in there sucked pretty bad" Knockers mused. They turned to see a throng of civilians, some of them armed, following them into the breach — a ragtag procession of poets, musicians, burlesque dancers, book readers and plain ol' pissed off residents who were arrested for being in the wrong place at the wrong time.

Back in the Golden Triangle district near the Clyfford Still museum, Pablo was applying a more persuasive form of compliance than his usual blast of weed smoke and poetry. He held a razor sharp tactical blade to the throat of a badly beaten dope dealer named Twitch whom he also had wrapped up in a half-nelson underarm choke hold. "I'm gonna ask one more time, you sorry little sack of bones, and then I'm gonna slit your throat and shove your own severed hands down your windpipe. What's the meth delivery protocol for EAR HQ?" The terrified tweeker finally relented "Th- there's a gate on the south end of the building where they know to look for my car. Th- they're always changing the code word but the new one is lu- lu- luna … I think. I mean I'm pretty sure of it. Please don't kill me."

"Yeah, you're sure of it." Pablo dropped Twitch to the ground, pulled out a joint, lit it and blew smoke in the guy's face while sending him off to nap town with a quick couplet.

Thanks for the intel and the car keys
I ever see you again I'll break both your knees

Pablo drove north in Twitch's car towards the EAR HQ

building that seemed to jut upward into the Denver moonlight like a steel spike. He pulled up to the south gate and stepped from the car, lifted the joint back to his lips and flicked his Zippo at the tip.

"Hey asshole, there's no smoking on the premises," yelled one of the EAR agents.

"Fuck you, cunt."

"What's the password?"

"Luna."

The gate opened and Pablo stepped through, whisking aside the lapels of his duster and switched on his amplifier and microphone while taking a drag from the joint. He exhaled and the whooshing sound of blowing smoke boomed through the speaker as an advancing cloud of THC wafted towards the back steps of the fortress.

Buck the fuck up, you drab little wrecks
I do not deliver I'm here to collect

His amplified words echoed forward and bounced back at his as he took a second hit and blew forth another mighty gust. Both sentinels on either side of the stone steps that led up to the back entrance began to freeze up with their rifles half raised.

Beware this fog you meth-addled minions
Your beloved demagogue who minces opinions
Has exposed you to fate perhaps premature
Yet it's far too late to forgive your tenure

The agents had been warned that Pablo Vasquez — The Soothsayer himself — would be planning some sort of assault and that they were to shoot on sight at anyone who posed a threat of any sort. Pablo considered their rifle positioning, interruption notwithstanding, to be cause for a grave act of self-defense. He pulled his pistol and shot a slug into the forehead of each agent who then crumpled with a thud. He took another pull and inhaled quickly — anticipating a wave of bad guys sent to answer his salvo — but they never showed up.

The echoes from Pablo's gunshots ricocheted about the stone-walled compound which quickly settled into an eerie quiet. Pablo looked up at the stone staircase that led to a steel door and began to postulate how much dynamite it would take to blow the thing in.

Electronic feedback fuzz from a loudspeaker above the door broke the silence. "Greetings visitor. Judging from how you treated our guards, I suppose it's safe to assume you do not have an appointment."

"Actually, I do. I have some unfinished business here. I would like to see Raul Geisel — otherwise known as Blatherskite. Can you send him out here to speak with me real quick?"

The speaker box crackled to life again. "I have been sent by Mr. Geisel to greet you. I can assure you that the firearm in your hand and the bomb strapped to your torso are not necessary. It is our intention to solve matters peacefully, to the satisfaction of all parties."

"First of all, you're full of shit and second of all, this is a speaker for amplifying my voice — same thing as you're talking through. Turn off your microphone and talk to me for real and I'll do the same."

The echoes from Pablo's amp and the sound of the EAR loudspeaker shutting off rippled about, and just as the area fell silent something in steel door clicked an it began to open.

A figure stepped forth and Pablo recognized the navy-blue coverall garb and military-style cap of an EAR agent.

Pablo tensed up and demanded "Who the fuck are you?" He relaxed a bit when he didn't see a weapon in the agents hands.

"I am," began the agent "the top-ranking member of an elite squadron of comrades under Blatherskite's command. Agent #1 of The Dinnermen — at your service." As he stepped into the moonlight at the edge of the top stair, Pablo nearly winced at the sight of a partially imploded husk of a face with receded eye sockets, sunken cheeks and deteriorating tissue around the nose and mouth. Agent #1 looked bad enough to gag a maggot on a gut wagon.

"Do meth much?" Pablo mused.

"We prefer to describe our emancipation from the vanities of the flesh through the miracle of narcotics as deconstructive epidermal minimalism. Our leader — the man you seek — has freed us from our digital addictions unto a far more powerful and eternal dependency of the biological sort."

"Bravo." Pablo pandered. "Delusional fanaticism and smack have always gone hand in hand."

"As a long-standing associate of the supreme leader of EAR, you have been selected to assist in the expansion of our enterprise from merely controlling the municipality of Denver to infiltrating the commercial nucleus of every major American city."

"In your dreams, motherfucker. Zip it with the sales pitch and take me to Blatherskite, now, or I'll mangle what's left of your ugly face."

As they ascended the elevator shaft towards the penthouse suite, Pablo kept Agent #1 in front of him to his right — watching for any sudden move that would warrant a bludgeoning.

"Your associate — the feisty young gal — she's safe and sound."

"Yes, I aim to confirm that."

"She was brought here as part of a plan to orchestrate a long overdue meeting between you and Mr. Geisel."

"Maybe long overdue but it'll be short and sweet," Pablo mumbled. He ran his right index finger along the curve of the pistol trigger and thought almost aloud, "Now that I have access to Blatherskite, I can dispatch this atrocity at any point." The elevator interior lights glowed a dim red as they rose further, at a slight diagonal pitch towards the top floor. Pablo placed a fresh joint between his teeth, switched on his amp and microphone, dropped his left hand into his duster pocket and thumbed his lighter.

When the elevator door opened, Agent #1 stepped out and two black conical hoses appeared from either side of the door and blasted white powder into Pablo's face at point blank. He reeled back in shock, the immediate sedation caused by the powder making him drop his gun and his joint while his microphone amplified his exasperation. Rather than containing sodium bicarbonate, the fire extinguisher canisters were filled with a modified recipe of MORE — mainly powdered Rohypnol with only trace amounts of meth, oxycontin and ecstasy.

"Beautiful shot, my Dinnermen! Although I like the ring of 'Agent #1' I believe my beloved title of Blatherskite suits me better. Please address me accordingly." The Dinnermen bowed in acknowledgement and dragged the semi-conscious Pablo to Blatherskite's desk which was positioned parallel to the west-facing wall of windows.

Bleary-eyed, stupefied and unable to move, Pablo gazed out at the lights of Denver as they stretched in glimmering lines across the South Platte River and climbed towards the foothills of the Rocky Mountains. It was a splendid and gorgeous sight save for the hideous face planted rudely in the middle of the scene. "After waiting so long to finally get my hands on you" Blatherskite quivered out of his blue coveralls to reveal a custom-tailored all-white Armani suit "I couldn't bear the thought of killing you quickly. My associates and I are going to savor this experience like a languid, seven-course meal and slowly devour you one morsel at a time."

"Is this where you killed her?" Pablo's words were like Laudanum slowly dripping through an IV tube.

"Who?" Blatherskite was coy.

"Luna."

"Oh, you mean the little snitch? Why, yes — as a matter of fact it is. I suppose that fact makes us special friends indeed. We've both eaten the same woman."

"Fuck you, Geisel. You're full of shit as usual."

"I am what I eat" he snickered. The comprehensive network of CCTV cameras throughout the EAR HQ building gave Blatherskite an abundance of footage of Luna's murder and subsequent devouring. He relished the opportunity to treat The Soothsayer to a last supper of sorts — a feast of video footage cut into a snuff film montage. Blatherskite touched a button on his desk and the wall of windows flickered into a giant video screen. Luna's assault, agony, demise and desecration were magnified to the 20th power and the only respite from the image was the necrotic, emaciated, cackling face of Blatherskite. Pablo was too weakened by sedation to look away, and although she had betrayed him, the sight of Luna being stabbed, slashed, bled and devoured cracked open a chasm of darkness and hatred in his heart that he never dreamed was possible. Pablo slipped into a stupor as the loop repeated across his glazed eyeballs and his microphone picked up the tiny, faint gasps from his mouth that uttered repeatedly, "No … no … no … no … no … no …

Far below in the basement detention block, news of the mayhem Earl and Knockers were whipping up a few blocks away had put the on-site personnel on high alert. Their poorly trained addict brains were bordering on panic mode which was a perfect distraction. Cricket was still perched atop the PVC pipe she was handcuffed to and had managed to coax the mini-shooter of *Granny Slapper Tequila* from her chest pocket. She whispered, "Always save one for later," then bit down on the lid and turned the bottle clockwise. She spit the cap away and sucked in the booze — welcoming the sting throughout her mouth as her salivary glands began to activate. She let the venom drool off her lower lip and onto the plastic just below her face.

The surface of the pipe began to melt, and Cricket aimed her drool in a line across the curve like a liquid laser. As the corrosion set in, she hoped the EAR agents would remain anxiously distracted from bathroom breaks, so she'd at least be dealing with a low-flow of sewage once the pipe split. "There's no way around it," she muttered. "I'm gonna get shit on tonight one way or another." She swung beneath the pipe and worked at the underside with less precise but equally effective globs of spit hawked upward with skill. She then maneuvered back on top, shimmied backwards a bit and waited for the pipe to crack. When it burst, she yanked the pipe to the right as the contents spewed onto the cell floor. After the initial expulsion, she slid her hands free of the cylinder but not without getting doused across the forearms. The stench made her gag as she jumped down to the floor while her pre-puking salivation kicked in. She rushed to the cell door and got there just in time to barf down between the bars onto the lock casing. Her saliva and stomach acid were enough to begin weakening the steel, but as before, she needed something else. "Goddammit Earl. Where the fuck are you?"

Chapter 42

Chemical Music

Beneath the embattled streets of Capitol Hill, Red-eye Robinson and The Whine-o were, according to their schematics, nearing the entry point. The dust, cobwebs and skittering floor dwellers had impacted the tenacity of both men — forcing them to dip into their respective libations for nerve-calming relief. Somewhere near the halfway point of their journey, Red-eye began absent-mindedly humming, which triggered Buster's incessant whining. Neither minded the idiosyncrasy of the other, and soon they began to harmonize while trudging along in the crumbling darkness until Red-eyes ears began to implode and The Whine-o's eyes were oases of tears. Then, they'd have to stop, shut up, comport themselves and forge onward — the whole process starting over again.

Red-eye watched the signal on his GPS locator increase in frequency, "OK Buster, we just passed beneath the garage, so just a few hundred more feet, and we'll be under the detention block." After couple more minutes of walking, Red-eye shined his flashlight upward at a cell floor drainage gate and down along the rungs of a rickety ladder. "Here," he said, handing the flashlight to Buster. "Shine this up there." Red-eye climbed the creaking rungs and began working at the hatch. He strained upwards and the old hinges held fast, the hatch giving Red-eye no lee way, just a face full of dust which prompted a tirade of hacking and swears. "Goddamn Pablo motherfucking Vasquez that cocksucking no good son of a dirty shit-eating whore," he coughed. "I swear on the mangled corpse of Jesus goddamn Christ I'm gonna kick his ass so bad he's gonna have to part his hair to take a shit." He lurched upward again, putting a hate-filled "ooomph" into it and the hatch finally creaked open — giving way to a musty holding cell in the far northwest corner of the EAR building.

Red-eye pulled Buster up into the dim cell, the sole source of visibility streaming across the floor through the jail door chow slot. Buster pulled at the door. "Dammit, man, it's locked. Now what?"

"No shit, it's a jail door not a grocery store entrance. That's why we brought this." Red-eye grabbed the butt of the Mossberg shotgun that was slung across Buster's back, pulled it free, held it up at face level and chambered a round. "I'd use the grenades, but I don't want to blow my own ass off trying to save someone else's."

Buster chuckled nervously, took a long pull of wine and then a deep breath. "OK, so what's the plan?"

Red-eye took a pensive sip at his bottle of *Badger's Breath*. "I'm gonna blast open that door and announce our arrival. A squadron of agents will come running this way to investigate the noise. You'll go out into the corridor, wait until they see you and then take off — drawing them after you. Once the coast is clear, I'll go find Cricket. You start making noise and keep moving, busting their eardrums with the highest-pitched whine you can muster. Find an exit and get the fuck out of Dodge."

"B ... B ... But -"

"But nothing. We've all got a role to play in this, and from where I'm standing that seems to be your charge. But hey, it's your choice. I'm going through that door, I'm gonna find our friend, and I'm gonna take out as many of these motherfuckers as possible in the process."

"OK." Buster sobbed. "Let's do it." He handed his sack of shotgun shells over to Red-eye.

"My man." Red-eye affirmed. They shook hands for an extra-long moment.

"Just one more thing." Red-eye warned. After I blast that door open and you hear those boots coming down the hallway, you'd better start crying. Cry like the goddamn wind."

Red-eye unloaded eight rounds of buckshot into the cell door lock casing in rapid succession. As the blasts sent noise waves flying down both directions of the cell block corridor, he kicked open the door for Buster. The Whine-o took a giant gulp of *Dago Red*, switched on his amp and microphone and stepped into the hallway while mustering a clench-fisted, lip-stained bawl. He started with a low, throaty tone that built steadily, bolstered by intermittent breaths and powered by an inherent proclivity for bellyaching protest. A squad of six EAR agents advanced toward him, closing in on his position as Red-eye reloaded in the shadows of the cell. The Whine-o retreated down the right-side wing of the corridor in a backwards wailing trot as his pursuers began wincing in aural pain mid-sprint.

As the EAR agents staggered past the mangled cell door holding their ears, Red-eye mused, "Damn, those fools look more fucked up than Buster." He waited for the herd to clamor down the corridor while listening for more advancing footfalls. He deciphered two sets of cautious feet and assumed they were coming to check the cell for other intruders. Not wanting to reveal his presence to the EAR populace at large, he unstrapped Pablo's nickel-plated ukulele from his back and hefted it by the neck, admiring its mass and compact size while addressing it with a whisper. "Now I know why that bastard sent you with me." When the pair of agents stepped into the cell, Red-eye allowed them to take a few steps in before bashing them each across the back of the head in an efficient overture of diagonal swings. He shouldered the shotgun, ran for the cell door, cut to the left and followed the corridor for several dozen yards. When he turned the next corner, he found himself face to face with the barrel of a Glock .45 automatic pistol clenched in the sweaty palm of Luther Fisk. "Come to serenade the maiden?" Sneered The Gasser.

"Uh, no. I'm just here to check the acoustics of the place. I'm playing the company Christmas party and doing a bit of preliminary research." The Gasser pulled his respirator down over his face and ripped out a vaporous rectal gag bomb. Before Red-eye knew it, he was passing out in a cloud of green smog.

Down the corridor beyond the wobbling legs of the laughing Gasser spanned a long row of holding cells that gave way to the basement mess hall. In the second to the last unit, Cricket was working furiously at the lock — probing at the keyhole with a bobby pin. The tequila in the *Granny Slapper* shooter had run its course by eating through the sewage pipe, and now she was faced with a denser obstacle.

Near the hallway's end, Red-eye Robinson was coming to — his eyes watering from the vapor cloud that had caused

his to slump down against the wall and black out. "Wake up, fucko," The Gasser taunted. "For a spook, well ... hah ... you sure do look scared all right!" Red-eye had a barrage of demeaning retorts queued up, but rather than return the insult he wisely refrained — although his mouth hung open at the sight of the reeking, jaw-grinding spectacle of unkempt human filth that wavered before him. He held fast to the ukulele as a last line of potential defense and The Gasser knelt and caressed the S-shaped curve of the instrument's body in a MORE-induced trance of delusion and wonder. "I love me some music," he garbled. "I'm gonna split your brain pan in half with a lead slug and slurp out your skull jelly, but before I do, I'd love it if you'd play me a tune. How about an ol' negro spiritual?"

"Don't mind if I do." Red-eye reached for his remaining bottle of *Badger's Breath*. The Gasser tensed up and pressed the barrel of the .45 directly against Red-eye's forehead. "It's OK, my man — I just need a little sip of the sing-sauce. It helps me relax." He took a long pull, swallowed hard, exhaled long, positioned the ukulele across his lap, switched on his microphone and amp and began to play.

The day the baby of my baby
Drowned down in darkened hell
She went a-skippin' 'mong the daisies
And tripped and fell into the well.

Down the corridor, Red-eye's wave of melody reached Cricket's ears and she began to sway unconsciously, dropping the bobby pin and clawing at the lock casing with her bare fingers.

Oh Lordy please save me
Help me find my little lady
You know I'm going plum crazy
About the baby of my baby

The tones were hypnotic, and Cricket felt the welling up of a deep-seated sadness. Although she was tough, she couldn't suppress it.

Every soul from the town
Even the hounds sick with rabies
Looked all around across the grounds
For the gift my life had gave me

Red-eye dug deep into his past, reliving the anguish once again — if only for the sake of the calamity at hand.

Oh Lordy please save me
Help me find my little lady
You know I'm going plum crazy
About the baby of my baby

The music seeped into the The Gasser's brain and immersed what remained of a person once named Luther Fisk — and for the first time in his life — he began to cry.

We found the baby of my baby
Stone dead cold and blue
You know the baby of my baby
Well she was my baby too

Meanwhile, the tears were brimming at Cricket's eyelids when she leaned forward into the jail door bars and let her anguish flow. The drops careened off the crests of her cheekbones, landed atop the lock casing and began to sizzle — eating through the steel like hydrated nitric acid.

Oh Lordy please save me
Help me find my little lady
You know I'm going plum crazy
Without the baby of my baby

At this point, The Gasser was in the throes of a complete emotional meltdown. Red-eye relentlessly strummed, starting back at the beginning of the saddest song he had even written, reducing Luther Fisk to a slumped over, blubbering basket case. Cricket's cage door clacked open in time with Red-eye's down strum and she stepped from the cell and began marching in time with the music towards her captor and her liberator.

The Gasser had plunged deep into an inner chasm of anguish, sorrow and desperate mania. "That's the prettiest song I ever heard about the thing I love the most — dead babies. All I ever wanted to do was to beat a mommy to death with her own strangled fetus. Is that asking too much of this ckickenshit child-worshipping world of whining snowflake candy-ass-" his rant was cut short as Cricket yanked her handcuff chain across his throat from behind.

"Tough shit, motherfucker," she growled, yanking him upwards and crushing his windpipe. "Once was too many, and now you're gonna pay." He popped out a fart and Cricket gagged, giving The Gasser just enough time to gain his footing and turn to face her while raising his pistol.

"Hey!" yelled Red-eye. The Gasser turned around again to face the barrel of a shotgun. "I'm glad you dig my music." Cricket whipped her hands up and over The Gasser's head and slipped deftly to the side as Red-eye got in one last word. "Sucker." He pulled the trigger and The Gasser's head blasted apart like a cantaloupe being thrown into the grill of an oncoming semi-truck.

As The Gasser's body dropped to its knees and faceplanted forward, it did what most mammalian biological systems do upon expiration. His final excretion sounded like a sousaphone tuba full of warm lard being huffed into in the middle of an earthquake. "Hurry let's go!" Cricket yelled, grabbing the Glock .45. "He's shitting his pants … it'll kill us both!" Red-eye leaped over the body and the duo sprinted from the rising green fume cloud which seemed to chase them down the corridor until they dashed into a stairwell and slammed the door behind them. "How the fuck did you get in here?" Cricket gasped.

"Tunnels. Pablo told us about a network of them running under Capitol Hill and Civic Center."

"Really? Incredible. That asshole has been trying to sell me that story for years. I always thought he was full of bullshit."

Chapter 43

Civic Disservice

Earl's high tolerance for alcohol served him well as he maintained a constant equilibrium of incoming beer and outgoing belches. He was getting drunk, but not sloppy. Instead, he was swept up in the heady rush of exacting destruction with impunity, which gave him a vigorous sense of euphoria he had never known before. He was imbued with the optimism of a liberty-smitten jailbird with a chip on his shoulder and loaded machine gun. He trotted towards Colfax Avenue, rounding the corner and heading westward with Knockers in tow and a few ex-captives following at a cautious distance. The self-proclaimed "Cleavage Beast" concealed her weapons beneath her trench coat as they slowed to a halt to marvel at an odd spectacle. Colfax Avenue — a street that would normally have been bustling with cars, buses, hobos, dealers, hustlers, hookers, hep cats and crazies — was deserted. The streetlights were dim and flickering and the only traffic in the lanes were bits of litter blown along by a light breeze. "This ain't right," Knockers warned.

"Yeah, this is downright weird" agreed Earl. They advanced towards Washington Street and then past Pearl Street as their briefly-emboldened throng of followers dissipated away from Colfax － either north into the Uptown district or south across Capitol Hill. "I better reload" whispered Earl as he stuck the tap in his mouth and sucked down into the lower half of the first keg. He thought he heard the faint idle of a diesel engine when a loud clunk pierced the night as a massive beam of light stunned them both into freeze-frame poses. An amplified voice boomed out, "This is Captain McClellan of the United States Army National Guard. You are being surrounded. Any sudden movements or attempts to escape will be met with a full-fledged military assault. You will not survive. You are advised to surrender immediately. Put your hands up."

"You ready?" Knockers murmured without moving her mouth. The tap was gripped between Earl's teeth, flowing a steady trickle of *Quasimodo Gold* into his mouth, over his bottom lip and down his chin. He kept gulping down mouthfuls of beer while raising his hands high. he managed to answer Knockers by gurgling "mmm hmmm." She followed suit by slowly raising her hands to the front, deftly pinching the loose fabric of the trench coat between each thumb and forefinger. She lifted her arms up and outward in a "V" formation — pulling the coat lapels away from the top curve of the magnifying glass so that each flap fell to the side as she let go and extended her arms.

"Hey, you," boomed Captain McClellan. "You on the left, drrrooooop yyyyooouuurrr …"

"Now," screamed Knockers. Earl spat out the tap, caught it and clicked it off while taking a massive deep breath. He squinted, clenched his fists and stepped forward, aiming for a point below the spotlight. He blasted forth a guttural cannonball that struck the spotlight Humvee. The vehicle was knocked back and skittered sideways, the jostling light beam revealed a phalanx of combat-ready soldiers frozen in position — transfixed by the hypnotic wonder of Knocker's magnified bosom.

The racket of the impacted vehicle threatened to jar the troops awake, so Knockers began a steady advance, pulling the cups of her brassiere slowly downward, revealing her areolas for an intensified effect. "Hold them in place," Earl yelled. "I'm gonna hit 'em again!" She continued forward, and like iron filings drawn to a magnet, the formation of stupefied slack-jawed soldiers began to lean forward towards her. She stopped and revealed her nipples, causing each man in the phalanx of testosterone-amped jarheads to orgasm uncontrollably inside their camouflage cargo pants.

Earl took another pull from the tap spout, swallowed hard and belch-blasted a lateral swipe from left to right that buckled the infantry ranks like a full-blast fire hose stream being swiped across a line of rickety fence pickets. Knockers punctuated the strike with a barrage of bullets while The Belcher used short, focused blasts aimed at enemy heads for maximum effect. Earl could see that they had breached the line and hollered "Let's go!" As they started to run, he stopped abruptly — Knockers nearly barreling him over. "What the fuck, ese? Vamanos!"

"Hang on." Earl looked at the awkwardly positioned Humvee, then up at the twin spires of the Cathedral Basilica of the Immaculate Conception towering in the background. He backed up three steps while sucking down beer, crouched low and took a running start at the vehicle while belching and righting his posture. With a "BLLUUUUUURRP" he catapulted the truck up and away. It sailed over Pennsylvania Street, flew high across the church parking lot and straight towards the east tower belfry. It struck the tower broadside in a three-ton explosion of motorized artillery smashing into a fortified column of concrete, iron, glass, wood, and steel. The impact collapsed the southeast belfry support column and the spire buckled diagonally and came to rest like the outward point of a broken finger. "Dios mio!" Knockers made the sign of the cross as Captain McClellan shouted out once again. "Stop right there, son. Or we'll blow your goddamn head off." Only now his voice wasn't amplified, and it seemed to waver a bit. Earl looked towards the shouting, and like an earthquake aftershock a belch blast flew from his gullet without effort or intention. Upon it rode his long-held, never expressed attitude towards authority. "FUCK YOU" he burped, in a guttural gust that sent Captain McClellan and a small cluster of remaining soldiers flying backwards up Colfax Avenue. "OK," Earl gasped at Knockers. "Now we can go."

They crossed to the south sidewalk of Colfax Avenue and continued west. At Grant Street, they veered left and headed towards the State Capitol building. As they approached the east lawn, an EAR van came skittering north across the grass from 14th Street while another Humvee careened down Colfax, cut across Grant Street and turned southward onto the green where both vehicles stopped front bumper to bumper a mere ten yards from Earl and Knockers. The soldier in the shotgun seat of the Humvee yelled, "Hey, remember The Captain's orders – do not stare at her tits!" His comrade yelled back, "Fuck you, man. That's the whole reason I followed them!" The EAR agents piled from the van with their AR-15s raised and Knockers went to work, whipping her trench coat lapels aside while being sure to stay just behind the Belcher's periphery. The squad halted like a herd of Keystone Cops — giving the object of their fixation ample time to shoot each of them in the face — including the driver —

who she managed to tag despite the windshield. Meanwhile, Earl used focused blasts like potatoes from a spud launcher to cranially incapacitate the soldiers. Simply out of disgust, he belched another blast of gut gas at the EAR van — sending it tumbling back towards 14th Avenue.

Emergency vehicle sirens and helicopter rotor blades sliced waves of alarm across the Civic Center grounds. Knockers and The Belcher were unfazed by the noise as they both gazed up at the glistening, majestic, gold-gilded dome of the Colorado State Capitol Building. Earl could feel Knockers looking at him. "Do it, ese," she dared with a grin. He drained the remainder of his right side keg, and this time he backed up a full half dozen steps, took a running start like a linebacker zeroing in on a quarterback and belched hard while thrusting his legs upward for vertical lift. The Humvee was flung up and outward in a high arc and began to rotate clockwise while remaining upright. It bashed into the golden Grecian curvature of the State Capitol dome back end first, mangling the gold leaf, the underlying copper plates and the structural limestone like a rusty knife jabbed into the upper curve of a Faberge egg.

"Bullseye motherfucker!" Knockers cheered while running for cover as a Denver Police Department helicopter pinpointed Earl with its spotlight. He followed Knockers beneath the canopy of trees along Grant Street and urged, "Help me with this" and she unfastened the empty keg from his harness so he could reach over his shoulder and pull it free. "Goddammit I gotta take a leak like never before," he thought as he took a swig from the other keg and stepped back out into the open.

A command boomed from the helicopter loudspeaker. "Drop the cannister or you will be fired upon!"

"Yo, Belcher, kill that fuckin' ghetto bird already!" screamed Knockers. He tossed the empty keg straight upwards against the downward rush of air and belched a direct, concentrated blast at the base of the cylinder — shooting it in a vertical trajectory directly into the helicopter rotor blades. The aircraft was jostled by the collision and began to waver as the pilot struggled to regain control. The chopper drifted sideways and careened into a tailspin that sent it into an updraft and then in a horizontal westward trajectory. It sailed over the defaced State Capitol, across Civic Center Park and directly into the stairway adorned, Roman column embellished, Neoclassical facade of the Denver City and County Building. The helicopter bashed into the structure in a whipping calamity of high velocity rotor blades smashing into marble, limestone, granite, brass and glass and then erupting into a gas-leak, spark-ignited explosion.

Chapter 44

Off with Your Face

One of the helicopter blades broke from the rotor upon impact. The dense ribbon of steel hit a flat slab of marble on the facade of the Denver City and County Building and was flung up at an angle to the south, directly towards the EAR building's northwest-facing wall of curved windows.

Inside the penthouse level, Blatherskite's deconstruction of Pablo Vasquez was mid-execution when the crash a block away jolted The Soothsayer from his stupor. He sat upright as the chopper blade crashed into the glass which shattered into a nerve-like network of interconnected fault lines. The impact cut the video feed of Luna's demise and broke the grip the gore had on Pablo's psyche.

Blatherskite's perfectly orchestrated vindication was jilted askew. "What the fuck!?" He shrieked.

As Pablo's neurology lit back to life, so too did his uncanny ability to metabolize chemicals. His constitution recognized the Rohypnol from back in the day before Arizona ditch weed was replaced by Colorado crippler. He used to lace his grass with the stuff on purpose — just to get more fucked up. The attention of his captors had been diverted, and he shook his head side to side violently while taking a series of deep breaths.

Blatherskite and the Dinnermen began scuttling about, fussing over the chopper blade that was stuck into the side of the building like a knife into a butcher block. Meanwhile, Pablo fished the last joint from his pocket, lipped it and checked his microphone and amp. They were still on, so he lit the joint, took a toke, exhaled and started to chant.

There ain't much time
And no such luck
I'm half out of my mind
And you're all the way fucked

He strained to enunciate through his narcotic brain-muck and exhale a thick cloud of THC across the penthouse floor. Blatherskite turned from the window where he was examining the chopper blade in time for the waft of paralysis to wash over his head.

I came here to face you
To settle an old score
I wanted to erase you
Now I want even more

As the Dinnermen and their speechless leader were suspended mid-frenzy, Pablo staggered back towards the elevator and found his pistol in the mitts of one of the ambushers. He shot the agent between the eyes along with his comrade, then strolled across the lens-like floor dispatching each of the remaining agents point blank — an indiscriminate one-man firing squad. He reloaded and again faced his old nemesis, his neurons fighting to connect along their time-tested, THC-forged pathways but diverting to new, uncharted, unsteady, MORE-manufactured routes. Murders that should have been deeply satisfying felt cheap and empty like a $10 hand job from a cockeyed Colfax hooker.

On the streets below, The Belcher and Knockers advanced on EAR Headquarters with cautious haste. They stopped at the EAR van Earl sent tumbling across the State Capitol lawn to assess their target. The van landed upright but was mangled in the melee and the front end had caught fire. Earl unzipped and relieved himself while putting out the flames. "You better be careful" warned Knockers. "Your piss might be flammable." Earl managed a chuckle while forcing his bladder to empty like a garden hose on full blast — knowing that McCallister was most likely regrouping and heading their way. He watched as a large puddle of *Quasimodo Gold* urine formed beneath the engine block and trickled downhill.

"Hey Knockers, I got it."

"Yeah, you got it all right."

"We're on the western slope of Capitol Hill. The EAR Headquarters building is a straight shot down 14th Avenue — three blocks from here. If you can get this thing into neutral, I'll belch you a shove and we can drive this heap straight through the front door of its home base."

"Well shit. I guess all beer drinkers ain't idiots after all."

Earl aimed a wide blast at the van's back bumper, and it shot forward as Knockers steered it back onto 14th and headed towards EAR. "Hurry up, motherfucker, train's leaving," she yelled. He raced to catch up with the van, amazed that he was chasing the momentum of his own belch to get into a vehicle that was used to try to kill him. He nearly caught up to it as Knockers navigated the slight curve around Civic Center Park and then aimed the front end at the double doors on the eastern curve of the ground floor.

Earl remembered the broken front window of the van and hollered, "Get down," from 20 yards behind. He sucked at his remaining keg tap as he ran, loading up for another fight while Knockers rammed the van through the front doors.

In the stairwell between the basement and the ground floor Cricket and Red-eye heard the crash. "That's Earl, I know it," she gasped, and started up the flight.

"Right behind you," answered Red-eye.

Meanwhile, Buster's caterwauling scamper had led him and his pack of pursuers to the far end of the basement level, at the auxiliary entrance to the garage. He was hell-bent on finding a way out of the curved colossus and back to his barstool at El Chapo. His bag of wine was almost empty, and between wails that held the EAR agents at bay, he drained the dregs of his *Dago Red*. The wine mixed with his mortal fear as he mustered his final high-pitched howl, which — to the MORE-deadened cochlea of the EAR agents was having an ever-diminishing effect. His las cry shrank to a whimper as his pursuers moved in towards him while he yanked at the locked garage door to no avail. "I hope you make it out, Red-eye," were his last words as the EAR agents hungrily riddled him with bullets.

Upstairs, the only way Earl could get inside was through the back of the van, as the width of the vehicle was the same as the double doors. He found Knockers slumped forward and bleeding from the throat, her trachea and left jugular sliced open by the magnifying glass that shattered when she hit the steering wheel upon impact with the building. Blood gushed from her throat as her vision blurred. Earl jammed his hand directly onto the wound to stop the bleeding. "Pinche

Belcher," she gurgled "vas a salvar a tu familia." Then, she went limp.

Red-eye grabbed Cricket's elbow, stopping her on the stairwell landing between floors. "There's a damn good chance we ain't gonna be able to just waltz out of this place like we're leaving the country club. Keep in mind now, the tunnels run directly below the basement corridors. I got in just down the hall from your cell."

"Good point."

"They don't know I'm here, so I'm gonna hang back and see if Buster shows up. You just get Earl and Knockers over here, and I'll lead us home guerilla style."

Knockers' demise plunged Earl into a fugue of anger and self-loathing remorse. The crash of the van had alerted every agent in the building except for the dead ones in the penthouse and those in the basement who were eating Buster. He paced outside the van in growling grief as the recently enlisted agents began filtering into the lobby from an acute semi-circle of entry points from the south, west and north. They began reluctantly raising their assault rifles towards Earl — waiting for one of the Dinnermen to tell them what to do. Earl sucked at what remained of his second keg of *Quasimodo Gold* with seething vigor and before any agent could get a shot off, he greeted them with a wide, dense wave of guttural rage. "FUCK YOU," he roared. The words rode atop the tsunami of gut gas like the jagged debris of a capsized cutter.

The stairway entrance was facing The Belcher. Cricket felt the blast of air and heard the knocking of skulls against the door. "I'm gonna wait until he stops to reload."

"I heard that" replied Red-eye. He considered the amount of noise Earl was making and calculated the seven rounds of buckshot left in his rifle against the six agents who'd gone shambling after The Whine-o. He ejected the empty shell and slid another into the chamber. "I think we're about to have some company from below. Speaking of company, where the fuck is Pablo?"

"How the hell should I know? If I had to guess, I'd say he's dealing with the asshole who runs this fucked up place."

Earl had knocked two dozen agents onto their backs. This time, rather than wait for the besmirched would-be gangsters to arise and begin firing, he mowed them down where they lay — emptying two full clips from his AR-15. "You assholes want to fuck around? Well, there you go." He realized he needed to stay on track and find Cricket. "Dammit, where the hell are you?" he muttered. High-octane beer, rueful death and the rush of gunfire murder had whipped him into a tight, staggering frenzy. He tried to call out for Cricket, but as before, the words got caught in the rising whirlwind of his guts and instead of a holler, out came "CRICKET" in a thunderous, rumbling belch.

She opened the stairwell door slowly, and as the echo of her name subsided, she answered. "Earl, over here."

He saw the stairwell door opening and watched, as if in slow motion, as Cricket emerged — a battered angel of steadfast grace. They ran to one another and met in the center of the lobby in a bittersweet, short-lived embrace. "Nice bracelets," Earl said, looking at her wrists.

"You wouldn't happen to have a handcuff key, would you?" As their lips met, a series of six shotgun blasts boomed from within the stairwell. " What the fuck is that?"

That's Red-eye in the stairwell. He's holding off an assault from a squad in the basement. That's also our way out."

Before Earl could answer, the screech of metal against glass shot through the lobby as the EAR van that was stuck in the entryway was yanked from its position by the winch on another National Guard Humvee. Several slabs of plate glass and a few rods of steel framing fell from the mangled facade, and after a moment of silence, Colonel McClellan strolled in. He was followed by a squadron of heavily-armed National Guardsmen (some with frontal stains on their khakis) along with the Denver Police Department SWAT team — decked out in full riot gear.

Cricket's cuffed hands were holding each side of EARL's face and she calmly reached to his left shoulder, grabbed the keg tap spout, placed it in his mouth and clicked it on.

Chapter 45

As Above, So Below

Regardless of the battle raging down in the lobby, Pablo carried on upstairs. He sat Blatherskite down in his chair and kicked it away from the desk — blowing out a pillar of pot smoke and pointing his pistol into the soulless grin of a putrefied swindler. "You know what, shitmouth," he began — checking the gun to make sure a round was chambered. "I hate music promoters" and then *BAM BAM* — Pablo dispensed a bullet into the top each of each foot and Blatherskite began yammering and blabbering uncontrollably like a crypt keeper speaking in tongues. "Also," Pablo continued, "I loathe government bureaucrats." *BAM BAM* — he sank two more slugs into Raul Geisel's guts. "And," he concluded, "I can't fucking stand tweekers." *BAM BAM* — Pablo shot two more times — once into each eye socket and Blatherskite's skull was blown into pieces. The lower jaw landed on the floor by the wall of windows and kept chattering and clacking away across the semi-translucent floor.

Downstairs, Colonel McClellan was smug and self-congratulatory. "Well, well Mr. manners," he began.

"It's Danners," Cricket corrected.

He continued unfazed. "Drop your weapons, walk away from one another, and we just might not execute you both right here on the spot."

She placed her hands back on either side of Earl's face, her back to the enemy — shielding him. "We're fucked," he gurgled, *Quasimodo Gold* trickling down his chin.

"It's OK" her voice was low and strong. "There's no place I'd rather be than fucked with you." Earl kept gulping at the keg, swallowing big and quickly finishing the last drop in the chamber. He spat out the tap, looked her in the eyes and smiled. They kissed long and deep like unrepentant sinners on the last train to damnation. She pulled back and a long band of saliva stretched between her lower lip and his. She smiled back and relished the face of an unsure youth who had become her spirited man.

She dropped the pistol and raised her cuffed hands, stepping slowly aside to buy some time. Earl closed his eyes, inhaled deeply and dropped his rifle. He raised his hands slowly as the soldiers and cops advanced. A low, catalytic rumbling swarmed inside him. He stepped forth with clenched fists, yanked his elbows backward and belched a deafening boom followed by a nanosecond of silence and followed by an explosion that threw Colonel McClellan, his troops and the SWAT team backwards against the inner wall of the building. Earl belched again, maiming bodies against impossibly sturdy I-beams which began to bend inward. As exterior reinforcements initiated another assault, the floor in the middle of the chamber exploded upward in an eruption of smoke, rubble and debris. It was immediately followed by another blast from further below.

They blinked in disbelief as the soldiers and cops strained to pinpoint them through the haze. "Yo, Belcher, hey Cricket," a voice sang from below. "It's Red-eye!"

Cricket grabbed Earl's hand, ran for the hole and jumped in, pulling Earl with her down into the basement. Just next to where they landed was another freshly-blown grenade hole. "Down here, hurry the fuck up," called Red-eye from the dusty muffle of the ancient Prohibition tunnel. They jumped in and ran behind Red-eye as National Guard and SWAT reinforcements filed into the EAR Headquarters lobby.

The support beams of the EAR building leaned inward, groaned and collapsed upon them in an avalanche of concrete, glass and steel.

Just as the girders were buckling inward, someone managed to escape the from the west exit dressed in blue EAR agent garb carrying a large satchel. The figure took cover behind an abandoned EAR van. A hand reached up to the side of the vehicle and traced an outline of the letter "L" next to E.A.R. "Sorry kid," Pablo muttered. "Never trust a musician."

The Belcher, Cricket, and Red-eye made their way several yards down the tunnel until they were stuck — blocked by debris knocked loose from the implosion of the EAR Headquarters building. "Fuck, man — what are we gonna do? I sure as shit can't sing us out of here," said Red-eye.

"I think I got us covered," offered Earl.

"But baby," gasped Cricket "You just ran out of beer."

Earl reached into his coat pocket and pulled out his lucky can of *Quasimodo Gold*, cracked it open and sucked it down.

Always save one for later.

About the Author

Luke Schmaltz was raised in Albuquerque, New Mexico and began writing poetry at the age of nine. He spent two-and-a-half decades writing, recording and performing with his punk rock band King Rat before embarking on a parallel career in fiction. He makes his living as a freelance writer and is a proud contributor to Modern Drunkard Magazine. He lives with his wife and their mutt somewhere in the Rocky Mountain region.